BROADWAY
CHANCES

BROADWAY
CHANCES

by
Elizabeth Starr Hill

VIKING

VIKING
Published by the Penguin Group
Viking Penguin, a division of Penguin Books USA Inc.,
375 Hudson Street, New York, New York 10014, U.S.A.
Penguin Books Ltd, 27 Wrights Lane, London W8 5TZ, England
Penguin Books Australia Ltd, Ringwood, Victoria, Australia
Penguin Books Canada Ltd, 10 Alcorn Avenue,
Toronto, Ontario, Canada M4V 3B2
Penguin Books (N.Z.) Ltd, 182–190 Wairau Road,
Auckland 10, New Zealand

Penguin Books Ltd, Registered Offices: Harmondsworth, Middlesex, England

First published in 1992 by Viking Penguin,
a division of Penguin Books USA Inc.

1 3 5 7 9 10 8 6 4 2

Library of Congress Cataloging-in-Publication Data
Hill, Elizabeth Starr,
Broadway chances / by Elizabeth Starr Hill.
p. cm.
Summary: In this sequel to "Street Dancer," twelve-year-old Fitzi, finally set-
tled into a normal life after years of street performances with her parents, gets
a chance to star in a Broadway musical.
ISBN 0-670-84197-8 :
[1. Entertainers—Fiction.   2. Family life—Fiction.   3. Musicals—
Fiction.   4. Theater—Fiction.]   I. Title.
PZ7.H5514Br   1992
[Fic]—dc20   91-42209   CIP   AC

Printed in the U.S.A.
Set in 11 pt. Bembo

BROADWAY
CHANCES

O N E

"At least the show had a pretty good run," Fitzi told her parents.

Mom responded with a rueful grin. "Only six months."

"We were hoping for something more like six years," Dad added.

He and Mom had just come home from an afternoon matinee. They had removed their stage makeup, but were still in costume. Both wore the white leotards that transformed them, for every performance of *Visions,* into garden statues; statues that came alive on cue, and mimed an eerie, enchanted dance.

Even to Fitzi, they looked oddly unreal, their graceful bodies so thin, their dark hair brushed down in stylized points on their foreheads. They drifted lightly into their chairs at the table, like moths coming to rest.

Fitzi went on putting out food for dinner. She, too, had hoped the off-Broadway play would go on forever.

Before *Visions,* she and her parents had worked as street dancers, miming and cartwheeling their way from one lean period to the next. They had taken whatever other acting, singing, or dancing jobs they could get.

During those years, they had moved so much, and Fitzi had worked so much, that she never could stay in regular school. Sometimes she was tutored, sometimes she attended professional children's classes.

But since January, thanks to her parents' steady work in *Visions,* she had stayed out of show business, except for one Crunchy Puffs TV commercial. She had been able to go to to P.S. 166, and had almost completed the sixth grade.

Well, she would get to finish the year, anyway. In two weeks, school would end for the summer.

"Soon *Visions* will be just part of our past. Just a line on the resume," Dad said moodily.

"But it did you a lot of good—professionally, I mean," Fitzi reminded him. The dancing mimes had been singled out for lots of special mention in the reviews.

"Well, now it's over," Dad sighed.

Fitzi opened cardboard cartons from the deli, and a box of Ritz crackers.

"Clement?" Mom called. "Want to eat?"

Clement Dale, Fitzi's grandfather, insisted everybody call him Clement; even Mom, his daughter. Even Fitzi, his granddaughter. "I have my own identity," he always said loftily when anybody commented on this.

In theatrical circles, Clement Dale was well known. Until last fall, when he had a stroke, he had worked more than forty years on the stage and in TV. Lately he had talked about working again, but hadn't gotten anything yet. Now, handsome and well-dressed as always, he strolled from his room and sat with the others at the table.

"What's this, my girl?" he asked Fitzi, peering into one of the cartons. "Culinary triumphs from Zabar's?"

She nodded. "Chicken salad." She slumped into her place between her parents. The three of them brooded in silence.

"I sense a certain undercurrent," Clement commented mildly. "Anything amiss?"

"The show's closing," Mom told him.

"Ah. Well, the box office had been falling off a bit, hadn't it?"

"We hoped for the best anyway," Dad answered.

"Of course, yes. Splendid show. Shame." Clement helped himself to chicken salad, adding, "Lance Harrington called a while ago. He had some news that might—"

Mom interrupted irritably, "Frankly, Clement, we don't care about Lance and his news right now. This family's in a terrible *mess* with the move coming up."

Fitzi realized this was true. Their sublease was ending,

and they were supposed to move into a large apartment in her friend Pip Logan's building. They could barely afford the new apartment, even with her parents appearing in *Visions*.

Mom's voice rose. "We can't possibly manage that high rent now! I don't know what we're going to do! Let's stick to our problems!"

"Yes. Right. Sorry." Fitzi's grandfather took a Ritz, gazing into space as though removing himself to another planet.

Lance Harrington was an old actor friend of his; actually, an old friend of the whole family. Fitzi wondered what his news could be.

They ate without speaking. When Mom got up to make coffee, Clement murmured, "I merely assumed Lance's call might bear on the present situation."

"Oh?" Dad asked, looking up. "What? How?"

Fitzi's grandfather mentioned a top Broadway producer who was casting a new musical. "Apparently it's going to be a mammoth production. Burt Janus and Monique Ormelle are set to play the leads. Tentative title is *Crowd Scene*. Huge chorus. Several featured bits for dancers and singers." Clement paused. "Lance is auditioning for it."

"No kidding! A show with Janus and Ormelle?" Mom spoke the names of the two well-known stars with awe.

Except for Fitzi's grandfather, who had been featured in a musical last year, no one in the family had ever had a part on Broadway. Lance Harrington, who was around

Clement's age, had wider experience, but hadn't worked at all in the past few years.

"You think he has a chance?" Dad asked.

"Well, *he* thinks so," Clement said. "The director called him personally—said one of the comedy routines might be perfect for him."

Mom and Dad exclaimed in excitement. "Super! Fantastic!" No matter how distraught they were, they couldn't help rejoicing in a friend's prospects.

"So he's trying out. And, incidentally"—Clement smoothed his mustache—"so am I. Apparently there's rather a nice bit for a stylish gentleman of vintage years."

"Hey! Wow! Terrific!" Mom and Dad both hugged him. Fitzi squealed with pleasure. Before his stroke, she had seen her grandfather in many plays, and she thought he was wonderful.

"Clement, you'll get the part," Mom said fervently. "I know you will." She and Dad exchanged glances. Their faces, pale and tense a few minutes ago, were bright with hope. If just one person in the family was working steadily—just one—they might be able to get by.

Fitzi felt a pang of sympathy for them, a love tinged with sadness. They wanted so much, expected so much. When she saw little kids going up to Santa at Christmas, she was always reminded of her parents.

·

Visions would be running for another week and a half, but there was never a performance on Monday. Fitzi's parents used the next Monday to job hunt.

Through friends, they lined up a crafts fair where they could do their dancing puppet act, and a restaurant that would pay Dad to go from table to table, performing magic tricks. He also got a gig for the opening of a gourmet grocery story, where he would juggle exotic fruit out on the sidewalk in front.

"Pray it doesn't rain," he entreated Fitzi and Clement at dinner that night, as he and Mom described these awful desperation-type jobs. They made the day sound funny, but Fitzi knew it hadn't been.

Dad burst into song: "Jugglin' in the rain—" He jumped up from his seat, tossed a few rye rolls into the air, then pretended to slip in a puddle. He caught the rolls deftly and returned to his seat.

Mom said, "Then, this afternoon, we saw Loretta." There was an odd note in her voice as she mentioned their agent. Fitzi noticed that she looked suddenly shy, almost embarrassed.

"Well, tell us what she said!" Clement demanded.

"She told us about the show you and Lance are trying out for, *Crowd Scene*," Mom continued. "She suggested— she suggested we try, too. For the chorus."

"Well, of course you should!" Clement agreed heartily.

"Absolutely!" Fitzi chimed in.

"I don't know." Mom shook her head. She rested her chin on her hand, her dark eyes lighted with dreams. *"Broadway,"* she murmured. Her face was rapt, as though she were seeing something she had looked for all her life.

"Broadway!" Dad affirmed, with his wide smile. He slapped his hands together. "It's showtime, folks!"

"I just don't need any rejection right now," Mom confessed. "I don't feel like risking it. We'd never get that lucky." She knocked on wood.

"Now listen, sweetheart," Dad said seriously, taking her hand, "if we can't absorb rejection, we're in the wrong business."

"Oh, I know, but—"

"What do we *have to do?*" Dad's gaze held hers intently.

"Keep trying," she admitted reluctantly, repeating the words they spoke about a thousand times a year. "Never give up."

"And what does that mean, in this case?"

Mom grinned and shrugged, surrendering. "Oh, okay . . . We'll go to the darned audition and give it our best shot."

"One never touches the stars without reaching for the sky," Clement contributed inspirationally.

"*Broadway*. That would be so *incredible*," Fitzi breathed.

"That's not all of it," Dad said triumphantly. "Loretta mentioned you, too, Fitz."

"Me?" Fitzi's heart began to thump.

"Uh-huh." It seemed that *Crowd Scene* was going to have more kids in it than any Broadway musical, ever. Many would have to dance and sing, and Fitzi was experienced at both. "So you'd have a good chance of making it into the chorus, anyway." Dad added, "Only if you want to, though. Understood?"

She nodded, overwhelmed. The subject of her working was a touchy one. She had objected so strenuously last year to staying in the street act with her parents, and had longed to attend P.S. 166 with her friends, Pip Logan and Karen Edman. So she had done that.

Next year, Karen and Pip would be going to some other school anyway. P.S. 166 only went through the sixth grade. Of course she had planned to go on with them, to junior high, but—

Broadway.

T W O

Fitzi and Pip watched as Karen cut out the pieces of the paper pattern. Neither of them knew much about sewing, but Karen and her mom were expert, and owned a good sewing machine. The three girls had bought cloth to make summer skirts.

"Voilà! Now we start pinning," Karen said. "Anybody else want to do that?"

"No," Fitzi and Pip agreed in one breath.

Mrs. Edman stuck her head in the door of Karen's room. "Need any help?"

Karen lifted her round freckled face and grinned at her

mother. Mrs. Edman joined the group, pulling up a chair to Karen's desk, where the cloth was spread out.

"You seem to be doing fine," she told her daughter. She pinned the pieces onto Fitzi's fabric. It was a vivid cotton print. "Yours is a teeny bit harder than the others," she told Fitzi. "We need to avoid cutting the giraffes in half."

The three girls giggled at this.

"Gosh, it'll be like a jigsaw puzzle, getting those pieces together," Pip said. "Maybe we should just have made headbands or something."

"It'll be easy," Mrs. Edman assured her comfortably. "You just match up the letters on the pattern. See? And Karen and I'll be right here to help."

Fitzi smoothed her giraffes, enjoying this simple afternoon. She hadn't told Karen and Pip she was going to try out for *Crowd Scene*. It was a separate part of her life, like a secret door opening. But she thought and thought about it.

She wondered if Tiffany Resnick would be trying out, too. Since the audition was an open call, items about it were sure to appear in *Billboard, Backstage, Variety*—all the trade papers. This meant that every possible candidate would show up for the first call. Tiffany was almost sure to be there.

Fitzi seldom saw Tiffany anymore, except in acrobatics class. For years they had run into each other a lot at auditions. Often they were up for the same part. Tiffany's sense of rivalry could be fierce, yet the years of shared experiences had drawn them into a kind of friendship.

Tiffany always knew the latest TV and theater gossip. She understood that shifting glittery world where most kids were outsiders.

•

Fitzi was a little late to acrobatics class. By the time she scrambled into her leotard and soft shoes, the others had lined up in one corner.

She ran into place behind Tiffany Resnick.

The piano player started the music. Tiffany peeled off in a long diagonal series of cartwheels across the room.

Fitzi followed. She had to hold back to keep from plowing into Tiffany, who was moving slower than usual.

"Take it again," the teacher called. "Fitzi, you lead this time." She moved Tiffany to the end of the line.

Fitzi saw Tiffany's angry flushed expression as they passed each other. For sheer motivation, nobody could get ahead of Tiffany, but she had gained a little weight recently. Her leotard hugged the new curves. That was probably what was slowing her down.

They repeated the long diagonal, did a few stretches, then practiced tumbling on the mat. At the break, Tiffany's bleached hair, tied up in a curly mass on top of her head, straggled in strands on her sweaty forehead. Wiping her face with a Kleenex, she sidled over to Fitzi and hissed, "Thanks a lot for making me look bad."

"I tried not to. You were *slow*," Fitzi protested.

Tiffany said in an angry whisper, "I've got my period. What do you expect?"

Fitzi wasn't menstruating yet. Covering her confusion, she merely said, "Oh."

As always, Tiffany's perceptions were fast and she went for the jugular. She rocked complacently, a hand on one hip. "I guess you wouldn't know, actually."

"Know?" Fitzi asked vaguely, wishing the music would start again.

"How it feels on the first day. I'm as sluggish as a log."

Fitzi couldn't resist asking, "Is this your first day ever?"

Tiffany's light laughter trilled at this absurdity. "Oh, of course not. I mean the first day every month. Of every period."

Fitzi longed to ask if she ever had accidents. Wearing a leotard—especially a white leotard, as her mother did each night in *Visions*—seemed so precarious. She knew tampons had to be the answer, but were they foolproof? Tiffany's smug expression made it impossible to ask.

Fitzi replied staunchly, "Sometimes my mom feels a little tired, but she always makes it to work."

Tiffany sighed, dropping her world-weary pose. "Well, I made it here, too," she answered, and took her position for the next set as the music began.

At the next break, she and Fitzi got paper cups of water at the cooler. Fitzi asked the question that had been on her mind all week. "Are you trying out for *Crowd Scene*?"

"Sure. That show's well named, half the town will be in it."

Fitzi said, "I'm trying, too."

"You!" Tiffany exclaimed in surprise. "I thought you didn't want to work anymore."

"Just for the chorus."

"How come?"

"Well, the school year's over, and—" Fitzi broke off and answered honestly, "I don't know how come. I miss it, I guess."

Tiffany nodded. Understanding flowed between them, rich with their memories. "Yeah."

■

Fitzi and her parents sat in a row, across their agent's desk. Steve and Donna Wolper wore identical black slacks and turtlenecks. Fitzi's clothes were the same, only red. All three of them kept their backs straight.

"Except for the leads, Janus and Ormelle, none of the adult parts are cast yet. They're going to audition for those right away, but kids' tryouts will begin after the end of school," Loretta explained.

Eager and tense, Mom asked, "Could you give us an idea of what the show's about?"

"It's the story of a group of French school children who steal a hot-air balloon and ride it to Paris," Loretta said. "The sets should be fabulous—the balloon, Paris streets and landmarks—"

"What happens in Paris?" Fitzi asked, fascinated.

"Basically, the country kids get involved with Parisian street life—plenty of opportunities for specialty numbers there, and featured bits for all ages." Loretta said there was a good part for a girl about Fitzi's age.

"Wait," Fitzi protested, her throat suddenly dry. "I wasn't thinking of a speaking part."

"Well, you're not likely to get one," Loretta replied tartly. "This is *Broadway,* dear. Anyway, they probably won't get to line readings in the first tryout."

"Oh, okay," Fitzi mumbled humbly. She just hoped she could be in the chorus and still keep up with junior high. If she actually passed the auditions. Which, of course, she probably wouldn't.

Her hands, clenched in her lap, relaxed a little.

·

Visions folded, unlamented. The audition for featured adult roles in *Crowd Scene* took place the following week. Clement easily won the part of Bistro Beau. Mom and Dad were offered a specialty number in their mime costumes, as part of the Parisian street scene. They would dance, mime, juggle, perform a few magic tricks.

This was more than they had expected, even in their soaring moments of optimism. As usual before an audition, they had thrown money into the Fountain of the Planets, on 49th Street, but had wished only to make it into the chorus. Now they were jubilant.

Their success, and Clement's, was cause for a first-class family celebration—especially as Bistro Beau shared a comedy routine with the Bartender, who was to be played by his friend Lance Harrington.

Lance went with them to dinner at The Personal Statement, one of their favorite restaurants. Catching Fitzi's eye across the table, he gave her a showy smile, his false teeth glinting in the candlelight. "Next we'll be rooting for *you, Fitz.*"

Mom reached under the table to knock on wood.

"When's your audition?" Lance went on.

Fitzi's stomach tightened. "Next week. Or at least the first one is. Loretta said there'll probably be three or four before all the kids are definitely cast."

Lance nodded. To her relief, he changed the subject. "Wonder if they'll have any dogs in the show. Haven't seen Bill Berloni for a while."

"Who's he?" Fitzi asked. Lance and her grandfather seemed to know everybody.

"Animal trainer. Trained the pup who played Sandy in *Annie,*" Lance told her.

Fitzi's grandfather commented, "What a life that animal had! Bill told me Sandy even had dinner at the White House."

"No!" Fitzi and Mom protested, laughing. "The White House?"

"Absolutely," Lance assured them solemnly. "Black tie. And he had his own standby, a pooch named Arf."

"Remember that cocktail party years ago, when Tallulah Bankhead brought her pet lion cub?" Fitzi's grandfather chuckled.

"Ah, yes. Winston, the cub's name was." Lance nodded.

"Whatever happened to Winston?" Clement wondered.

"He got too big to go to parties, so Tallulah gave him to the Bronx Zoo."

"Tough, for a party animal."

The two old men bounced stories and jokes off each other, as they always did. Fitzi listened happily, eating buttery garlic bread. She finished off two pieces with her lasagna. Usually the family ate very low calorie food to stay trim, so this was a huge treat.

Her grandfather raised his wine glass. "Here's to us! May we always have cause to celebrate!"

THREE

The day of Fitzi's audition coincided with the family's move to the new apartment. They always rented furnished places. Except for clothes and books, Clement's record collection, and Fitzi's dollhouse, there wasn't much to take.

The family decided that since their new home was just a few blocks away, the easiest thing would be to take their stuff over in one or two cab trips. Mom and Dad could do this while Fitzi's grandfather took her to the audition.

On the afternoon before, Fitzi took her books from the shelf in the living room and stacked them in boxes in her room. Moving always made her feel forlorn. The family had knocked around so much.

This room had been hers for less than a year, yet she had lived here longer than anyplace else. As she looked around, the space seemed crowded with the ghosts of other rooms, different walls and pictures and curtains, homes settled into and soon left behind.

She hadn't packed her notebook yet, and sat down on the bed to write in it. "Tomorrow we're moving and I'm trying out for *Crowd Scene*."

The sentence seemed so freighted with importance that she couldn't write anymore. She closed the notebook.

By the window, the avocado plant held a glimmer of sunshine in its green leaves. It had grown taller; last year, the sun never reached it till late afternoon. Fitzi imagined it stretching, growing, even as she watched. It belonged to the owners of the apartment, but she had taken care of it all this time. Now it would be theirs again.

So little was definitely, permanently hers.

Unhappy and out of sorts, she went into the living room and flopped into a chair. Clement was on the phone, shouting ill-temperedly at Peppy Pete's about their overdue lunch order: "Then send a peppier delivery boy! We're *hungry!*"

Dad was piling the makeup kits and his magic gear near the door. Mom got a Sundance Sparkler from the fridge and drank it quickly, her thin face smudged with dirt, black leotards and tights dusty. "Whew, what a hassle," she sighed. "I hate moving."

Dad stopped to rub her neck. "Lot of tension there," he told her. "Better take a breather, hon."

Mom nodded, went over to her exercise mat and stood on her head, sending energy to her brain.

Clement banged down the phone and strode away from it, roaring, "*Idiots* are running the world now!"

The downstairs buzzer rang, and, after Fitzi pressed it, the doorbell. It was Pip, fair hair gleaming like honey in a braid over her shoulder. In her funny crackling voice, she offered, "If you'd like somebody to make a mess of your packing, ask me to help."

Fitzi broke out laughing.

Pip followed her into her room. "Gee, it's pretty bare."

"Yeah."

"Looks like you're almost done."

"Yeah."

On top of a packed box of books was *The Rendells at Sea,* which Pip had given her for her birthday last fall. Recognizing the cover—a burning ship sinking in a vivid green ocean—Pip smiled. "Wasn't that an awesome story?"

"The best."

"*The Rendells in the Haunted Car* may be the *absolute* best."

Fitzi's heart lightened. It would be fun living in the same building with Pip.

"What time are you moving in?"

Fitzi still hadn't mentioned the audition to her, or to any

of her other school friends. For one thing, it would be awful having to tell them if she bombed out.

"I'm not sure," she said.

.

The next day, Fitzi and her grandfather got to the audition early. Already a line of kids, most with parents, was waiting to get into the theater. A newspaper photographer was snapping pictures while a reporter interviewed members of the line.

Fitzi saw Tiffany lean over a younger child's head to thrust herself into camera range. She announced loudly, "My name is *Tiffany Resnick*. I began my career in a *Petal Soap ad*. My hobby is *ice skating*."

Another girl bleated meekly, "I'm a natural singer. I just seem to have a natural gift."

Mothers elbowed each other aside to state their daughters' names, ages, and outlook on show business: "We've never pushed her, she's just doing what she loves," was a popular theme. One asserted, "Alix has appeared in forty-one TV commercials, but we make sure she leads a normal life. That name is spelled A-l-i-x."

Only girls were to try out today. Boys in this age range, and younger children, would be tested separately. Parents and agents had been warned that the girls had to be between ten and fourteen, no taller than four feet ten. But Fitzi could see that many of the girls were too tall, even slumping and bending their knees. She was safe, but wondered about Tiffany, who topped her by an inch or so.

The doors opened, and kids and parents streamed inside.

As they entered the theater, Fitzi saw a rope stretched across the stage. "Four feet ten?" she whispered to her grandfather.

He nodded, his sharp blue eyes amused. "Keeps you honest."

"Okay, young ladies, take seats in the front rows," a heavy-shouldered, rumpled man called from the stage. With a tingle of awe, Fitzi recognized Seymour Ettl, the show's director, a Broadway veteran with a long list of hits to his credit.

Her grandfather murmured, "Break a leg, kiddo," and took a seat in the back of the theater.

Fitzi sat with some other kids in the second row. Tiffany bustled into the first row, directly under Mr. Ettl's feet—the only contender to sit so far forward.

"Ted'll sign you in," Mr. Ettl said.

Ted, the director's assistant, took everybody's name and gave each of them a cardboard number. "Hold on to that," he told them.

The numbers went from one to sixty-four; Fitzi's was nineteen. Nervousness spiraled tight inside her. Was nineteen a lucky number?

She wasn't sure. Maybe she should try to swap with the runty, scared-looking kid sitting next to her, who had number seven. She put it to the kid, who drew away, muttering, "Leave me alone."

"Okay, please come onstage now and line up in front of the rope." Mr. Ettl gestured to where they should stand.

Tiffany bounded up the stairs to the stage ahead of the

rest. She walked confidently to the rope. Fitzi was glad to see that it cleared her blonde curls.

Fitzi took a place beside her. She had never stood on a Broadway stage before, even in an audition. The houselights were on, and the theater seemed enormous. Her grandfather, way in the back, was toylike, but she saw him wave.

Seymour Ettl walked past the line, his head thrust forward like a turtle's from those heavy shoulders, looking the girls over. Fitzi felt suddenly meager, glaringly aware of her brief flip of dark hair, thin big-eyed face, bony body. She wished she hadn't chosen to stand next to Tiffany, who preened lushly beside her.

At last Mr. Ettl asked the group sympathetically, "Isn't it depressing, being told what height you should be? But it's necessary." He went down the line calling out the numbers of each too-tall girl, while his assistant checked them off the list. "Thank you." Mr. Ettl dismissed them.

Mentally Fitzi started counting; about a dozen were out.

"Now Ted's going to show you a little dance sequence and ask you to hoof it, right here on the spot."

His assistant demonstrated a series of steps, while a weary-looking pianist played a few measures in the orchestra pit. Fitzi saw the steps were simple. Repeating them with the other girls, she had no trouble duplicating the sequence or sticking to the beat.

When they got to the final turn, several girls were out of step. One or two were so rattled that they dropped their number cards. Again Mr. Ettl thanked and dismissed a dozen or so.

Then it got harder. Ted broke them into groups of four girls each, and the sequences they were asked to repeat were more difficult.

By the time they reached Fitzi's group, she was sweating with apprehension, but she performed her steps flawlessly. Tiffany's group was right after hers; Tiffany kicked off like a popping champagne cork. Powerfully and accurately, she outdanced everybody in her foursome.

When the last contenders were finally done, Mr. Ettl said, "I wish I could use every one of you. But—" Again he called out numbers, thanked some girls and let them go.

Fitzi and Tiffany ended standing next to each other. They exchanged happy smiles.

"Now I'm going to ask you to sing a song you all know," Mr. Ettl said. He added jocularly, "At least I hope you do. It's 'Happy Birthday.' Anybody not familiar with that?"

Everybody giggled obligingly.

"My name's Seymour. You can make me the birthday boy."

Again, polite giggles.

"I'll listen to you one at a time." His tone got weightier. "I warn you, you're going to have to hit the high F-sharp. Please, if you can't do that, don't waste your energy and ours."

Number seven burst into tears and ran from the stage.

Fitzi's throat clutched up. Her singing was weaker than her dancing, and she wasn't sure she could make that note. But if she didn't try, she was out for sure. She breathed slowly, as her father always urged her to do in extreme stress, and tried to think calming thoughts. She visualized Dad's favorite: a smooth white egg.

Ted herded them into the wings and called them out one by one. As each applicant went for the F-sharp, Fitzi began to hear a fuzzy droning in her ears. Maybe she was about to faint. She could hear many of the singers going flat at the crucial instant, or thinning to a wobble. "Happy *bi-i-irth*-day, dear Seymour—"

"Nineteen, please."

Fitzi took an extra long breath and marched to center stage. She held her number in front of her chest and pasted a smile on her face.

The piano accompaniment started again. The first couple of happy birthdays flowed out of her easily enough. The third one, the one with the high note, was getting closer. And the droning sound in her ears seemed louder. Alone in this beehive of faintness, she searched the rear rows of the orchestra for her grandfather.

Her eyes found him. A steeliness forged between them, as if the force of his will gave her strength. She swung into the third happy birthday, and hit the F-sharp right out of the ballpark, clear and true.

FOUR

"**F**rom now on, your nickname is Leather Lungs," Fitzi's grandfather announced, his blue eyes twinkling. He and Fitzi sat with Mom and Dad on still-packed boxes in the new apartment, relating the afternoon's triumph.

"What about the other kids who were left at the end?" Mom asked. In rumpled slacks and an old shirt, she was tired from the day of moving, but eager for every detail. "Anybody good?"

"There was one ripe little blonde, out for attention every second." Clement laughed. "High energy level. Chutzpah."

"But can she sing and dance?" Mom demanded. "Or was she just upstaging everybody?"

"Both," Clement responded. "Definitely competition."

Fitzi asked, "What number was she?"

"Six."

"That was Tiffany. You know her, Mom. Tiffany Resnick, from acrobatics class? You've seen her at lots of auditions."

"Oh, yeah." Mom's brow clouded. "So what are you saying, Clement? That number six upstaged everybody else?"

Sensing trouble on the way, Dad jumped to his feet. "How about we eat out tonight? We've got no food and the place is a mess, so—"

"I don't have the strength." Mom sighed.

"Fine. Okay." Dad gave his wife a wide smile and a kiss. "I'll bring back sandwiches. Ciao." He was out the door.

"Sounds as if this Tiffany Resnick mugged a lot and was a real distraction," Mom told Clement in a tone of exhausted resignation.

Fitzi put in, "Mom, remember I'm just out for the chorus. Tiffany's out for blood."

Mom started on the topic of unfair tactics and unprofessional kids, a favorite complaint of hers when she feared somebody might have beaten Fitzi out in an audition. After a few minutes, Fitzi slid unobtrusively into her new room, leaving her grandfather to cope with Mom. She shut the door softly behind her.

Her room. This was her room now.

It was smaller than her last one, painted pale peachy pink, like the inside of a shell. Her dollhouse was in a corner. There was a desk, a bookshelf.

Fitzi looked out the open window. The apartment was on the fifth floor, and her room was in the rear of the building. She couldn't see much, except the rusty iron fire escape across the alley. It had four dusty plants on it, and several pigeons.

The wide sill of her window was whitened with pigeon droppings. They must come over here, too, sometimes.

Her mind stirred with warm, hospitable plans. As soon as Mom and Dad bought some Ritz crackers, she would put out crumbs for the birds. She would encourage them to hang around. Maybe they would build a nest on the fire escape. When the baby birds hatched, they would know they could always get a meal right here, on Fitzi's sill.

She sat, dreaming, until dusk seeped into the summer evening, dimming her view. Then she closed her eyes tight, and took in the unaccustomed sounds. The traffic noise was muted on this side of the building. It made a distant dissonance, threaded with radios, TV voices, a baby's cry. By listening with all her might, Fitzi could catch the whirring coos of the pigeons.

When Dad returned with food, she ate a sandwich and unpacked her books. Soon the bookshelf was bright with the familiar covers. She unearthed her notebook, sat on the bed, and turned to yesterday's entry: "Tomorrow we're moving and I'm trying out for *Crowd Scene*."

After it she wrote, "We've moved. Our apartment is on the fifth floor. The elevator rattles."

She followed that with a much longer description of today's audition, including everything she wanted to remember—the springy feel of the stage floor when she danced, the high F-sharp, the glorious fact that she had made the first cut and would be called back for the next tryout.

Even if she washed out later, she had done well to get this far. She decided to tell Pip and Karen about it.

.

Next afternoon, Fitzi went to Karen's to work on the skirts they were making. Pip was already there, bent over the sewing machine, the tip of her tongue protruding between her teeth as she concentrated on sewing a straight seam. The needle of the machine clacked slowly in and out of the cloth.

"It's puckering," she said tensely.

"Wait." Karen freed the cloth and straightened it. "There."

Fitzi sat down and watched for a minute. Then she cleared her throat. "May I have your attention, folks? Big announcement here."

"You're moving again," Pip said absently.

"Touring the country for Crunchy Puffs," Karen guessed. Then, noticing a hazard, she told Pip, "Don't put your finger under the needle, *ever*."

"This really is important," Fitzi said meekly.

"Okay, let's hear it." Karen pushed her red hair back and cupped her ears.

"Ta-dah!" Pip trumpeted.

Fitzi launched into her long explanation. Both girls listened raptly. When she had finished, they shrieked and hugged her. The sewing was forgotten.

After they had asked a dozen questions, Pip said in mock reproach, "I can't believe you went through a major event without breathing a word to us."

Fitzi knew she wasn't entirely joking. The threesome usually shared ideas and plans. It was rare for one of them to make even a trivial decision without consulting the others.

Yet even now, basking in their friendship, Fitzi felt herself pulling away from them, with a mixture of regret and restlessness. In a parody of penitence, she covered her face with her hands. "I'm so ashamed."

Karen asked seriously, "What about junior high? We promised to go on being best friends in junior high."

"Yes. And we *will*," Fitzi vowed. "First of all, I probably won't get into the show."

Pip and Karen protested loyally.

Fitzi went on, "Even if I do, a lot can go wrong. It might bomb and fold right away. Besides—if I don't start regular school in September, I'll be tutored, so I can join your class late, if I have to. But honestly," she added, "it'll probably be over for me after another round."

∎

Loretta phoned to confirm the day and time of the next audition, and to say that Mr. Ettl wanted to hear Fitzi sing again—a different song this time.

"He must have really appreciated that F-sharp," her grandfather commented when Dad got off the phone.

"Sing what?" Fitzi called.

"A real oldie called 'The Travelin' Life,' " Dad told her. "It won't actually be in the show, it's just a test piece."

"Ah, yes." Clement hummed a few bars. "Liza Minnelli sang that at the Palladium when she was a youngster. In 1964, I believe. Not a bad choice for an audition. Lots of youthful bounce."

Fitzi protested, "I've never even heard of 'The Travelin' Life.' I can't do it."

"Of course you can do it," Dad said firmly. "I'll pick up the sheet music from Loretta this afternoon."

"Good," Mom said fervently. "When's the tryout?"

"Friday."

"Tell us exactly what she said," Mom begged Dad, pink-faced with excitement.

"Well, you know Loretta. She doesn't give away much." But Dad's puckish grin showed he was pleased. "They want Fitzi to dance again, too. Tap shoes this time."

Fitzi had a peculiar feeling, as though someone else were being discussed. Tap shoes. A different song. She said faintly, "I was just trying for the chorus."

"Lance can teach her the song. He's got a piano at his place," Clement reminded them.

"Aren't these kids in the play supposed to be French?"

Fitzi asked desperately. "Will I have to work up an accent, too?"

"Don't get lost on that," Dad told her impatiently. "If they wanted French kids, they'd have gotten French kids."

"Just give the lyrics kind of a lilt," Mom advised.

"I don't see why they couldn't ask us to sing 'Tomorrow,'" Fitzi complained. "Everybody knows 'Tomorrow.'" The song from *Annie* had been a staple at auditions for years.

"Better to hit it fresh," Mom said enthusiastically. "Different song, new interpretation."

"I just can't do it."

"You can."

■

On Friday, Fitzi was back onstage in her tap shoes, with Seymour Ettl, Tiffany, and the other girls who had survived last time, along with a group of boys who had tried out separately. Everybody had signed in, and each held number cards again.

The height rope was gone. Some of the boys were older and taller than the girls. One head of brown hair rose above the others.

With a lurch of dismay, Fitzi recognized Mark Hiller, a teenage veteran of the TV soap opera she and Tiffany had tried out for last year. She had been terrible at that audition, and had fled in tears. Mark, a couple of years older than she was and a skilled actor, had witnessed her shame. She just hoped he wouldn't remember her.

Seymour Ettl greeted the contenders and introduced

them to the show's composer and choreographer, who were seated in the front row. The presence of these famous men, ready to test and judge, heightened Fitzi's tension. She glanced at Tiffany, who was standing beside her. For once, Tiffany's face was rigid and grave.

"We already know you can dance, but we're going to make it a little harder today." Mr. Ettl beckoned to Ted, who demonstrated a long sequence, ending with a triple-time step. His taps echoed through the theater in a stuttering series, frighteningly fast. When the kids had to follow him, Fitzi heard some faltering slightly, clacking out of sync. But even through the triple-time step, she never lost the beat, nor did Tiffany.

"Okay," Mr. Ettl said noncommittally when they were done. The men conferred. Ted made notes.

Then they went on to the singing. Boys performed first, one at a time. Their song was "Leaning on a Lamppost." Together in the wings, Fitzi and Tiffany watched and listened. Nobody seemed to bring anything special to the song—until Mark Hiller, holding his cardboard number nonchalantly under his arm, strolled jauntily to the center of the stage.

"Look! It's that cute guy on *Inner Tempest!*" Tiffany hissed.

"I know. Shut up," Fitzi whispered.

Mark leaned in the air, against an invisible lamppost, and tossed out the lyrics as naturally as if they were his own thoughts. He was so believable, so alive, that Fitzi felt like clapping when he was done. She forgot she had hoped he wouldn't notice her; forgot everything except the thrill of seeing someone perform so well.

As he came offstage, she grabbed his sleeve and whispered, "You were wonderful."

"Thank you." He looked slightly surprised. "I thought you were going to hide from me."

Fitzi drew back, embarrassed. She realized he knew just how she had felt before. She wished she hadn't spoken to him.

Prickling and discomfited, she waited for her number to be called. Gradually her concentration returned as one girl after another belted out the words and music Lance had dinned into her. Some used a French accent.

To Fitzi, Tiffany seemed the best. She had a bounce and sparkle nobody else could match.

Fitzi's number was called next. She bit her lip, hating to have to follow Tiffany; hating to risk failing in front of Mark. For a wild moment, she thought of escaping now, while she could; running backstage and away. But, propelled by pride, she strode to center stage, sang the song as she had practiced it, and exited off the other side. She had no idea whether she had done well or badly.

FIVE

The audition ended shortly afterward. As Fitzi ran down the side steps from the stage to join her grandfather, she saw Mark Hiller watching her, his lean face enigmatic. She turned away.

She caught up with Tiffany. Neither girl spoke. They were both wiped out. They trudged up the aisle and parted near the back of the theater, where Clement was waiting.

"I was proud of you, my girl."

"Good." It was hot outside, a humid New York day. The sky seemed low and whitish, gritty. Little whirlwinds of dust spun across the pavement.

Her grandfather suggested, "Let's stop and have lunch. And a cold drink. That was a long, thirsty audition."

Fitzi agreed gratefully. Since it was past the usual lunch hour, they were able to get a roomy booth in a coffee shop.

Over lunch, her grandfather gave her a detailed analysis of the tryout, praising her own work, criticizing some of the others. "One young fellow, I've seen him on TV—in *The Inner Tempest,* I think—"

"Yes. Mark Hiller."

"Excellent. Not a great singing voice, but he gave the song such charm. And he's a fine dancer."

"Is he? I couldn't pay much attention to him when we were dancing."

"You amazed me with that triple-time step."

"Mom taught it to me last year, but I've never practiced it much."

"Shirley Temple used to do a triple-time step."

Fitzi listened absentmindedly as her grandfather talked about the child star of long ago. She wished they could go on talking about Mark.

Still on Shirley Temple, her grandfather continued, "Star quality changes. I doubt if that gruff-voiced tot would get far today, with her rolling eyes and her pout."

"What? Oh. Maybe she just did what people wanted."

"Maybe. Anyway, you were one of the few who carried off the triple-time step."

"Tiffany did, too. And she sang better than any of the rest of us."

"Yes, the little blonde has luster. No doubt about it. However, you have your own appeal."

She put down her sandwich. "Do I?"

He nodded. "There's always something going on in your head, Fitzi. That shows. It's interesting."

"Do you think I'll make the chorus?"

"I'm fairly sure you will. In fact, you may get a featured bit." He rapped a finger against his coffee cup, measuring his words. "*If* you want one. I'm not sure you do. With your parents and me set for the show, there's no financial pressure. You could just go on to junior high with your friends, as you planned."

"I suppose so."

He looked at her, puzzled. She kept her eyes on her plate.

•

Loretta reported that Fitzi had made the second cut, and was being asked to read for a speaking part. The agent said she couldn't guess exactly what Seymour Ettl had in mind for Fitzi. Probably he wouldn't know himself, until he heard her read.

After the agent's call, Fitzi was in a turmoil. Her parents reacted so excitedly that she wasn't sure how she felt. As soon as she could escape from them, she ran downstairs to the fourth floor, and rang the Logans' bell.

Pip answered the door, loosing a blast of a New Kids album into the hall. Usually she looked completely welcoming; nothing complicated about Pip. Now, though, her "hi" was slightly constrained.

Karen was behind her. "Just in time for the fashion show." She twirled awkwardly. Both were wearing the skirts they had made.

Too late, Fitzi remembered she had been supposed to go over to Karen's yesterday and finish off hers, too. Feeling guilty, she followed them into the living room.

Pip's zipper had been sewn in crookedly. The skirt didn't hang straight. Karen's was perfect, but its fullness made her seem plumper than ever. They paraded past Fitzi, making an obvious effort to act exactly as usual.

"Listen. I'm sorry I missed yesterday," she said.

Pip turned the stereo down. Her averted gaze, the stiff way she moved, reinforced Fitzi's impression that she was upset.

"So." Karen sat on the sofa, next to Pip. "What's been going on?"

Ill at ease, Fitzi lowered herself into a chair. She described the last audition, putting in explanations of everything they didn't understand.

She found it hard to define her problem. The jumble of details assumed, as they poured out, a glamour she hadn't intended. Long before she got to Loretta's call, Karen and Pip wore glassy, guarded expressions.

With a sinking heart, Fitzi remembered a silly character in the Rendells of Rawling books—wealthy Aurora. Aurora was always complaining that her diamonds needed cleaning. Now it seemed just as idiotic to complain about being seriously considered for a real part in a Broadway play.

Lamely, she wrapped it up with, "Anyway, I got

through again." She asked Karen how she had made the cute pockets on her skirt; they were shaped like poodles.

Relieved, Pip and Karen jumped into the change of subject. They brought out a Simplicity pattern book; Karen's mom had offered to help them make dresses next. They had picked out four with possibilities, which one did Fitzi like best?

She chose one; Pip argued for another. Karen, who had trouble with decisions of any kind, complained, "I'm torn. I'm torn. Maybe we should try pleats. Or . . . "

•

As soon as Fitzi got home, she called Tiffany. "I made the cut."

"So did I."

"I knew you would."

Never tactful, Tiffany replied, "I wasn't so sure about you."

"Gee, hold the compliments, I can't take too much at once."

"You did the song as if you were mailing it in. What happened?"

"Look, *I made the cut.* It can't have been that bad."

"I didn't say it was bad."

"My grandfather liked Mark Hiller."

Tiffany laughed. "Who wouldn't?"

"He doesn't have much voice."

"He doesn't need it."

There was a pause. Swallowing, Fitzi admitted, "I'm scared, Tiffany."

Silence. Sympathy wasn't Tiffany's strong point, but Fitzi rushed on, "It's like—I feel as if I'm in over my head, like drowning."

There was another silence. Then Tiffany said, "Well, see you at the reading."

Fitzi sighed. "I guess so."

S I X

The reading was held in a rehearsal room, bare except for some scattered chairs and a piano in one corner. Fitzi's mom went with her.

Seymour Ettl, smoking a cigarette and looking tenser than he had at the other tryouts, stood at one side of the room, chatting with three or four men. On the other side, an equally tense cluster of kids talked quietly. There were just four girls around Fitzi's age, four teenage boys including Mark, and three small boys.

Fitzi had never seen these little boys before. Nervous

herself, she was sorry for them, wondering if they felt even worse than she did.

Mark was bending slightly, nodding and listening to one of them. The boy was no more than six or seven, his upturned face earnest. Mark's gravity, his attentiveness, tugged at Fitzi. He glanced toward the door and saw her. Hastily she looked away.

Ted, Mr. Ettl's assistant, signed Fitzi in; there were no numbers today. Mom whispered, "Break a leg, sweetie," and took a seat with some other parents.

Tiffany came in a minute later, alone. As she joined the group of contenders, her gaze swept over Mr. Ettl and the other men across the room. It was as if a searchlight had passed across them; all eyes flickered to her.

Fitzi felt a pinch of envy. Mark, too, was looking at Tiffany. She was not especially pretty, no prettier than Fitzi, and less so than many of the girls who had been discarded in the first tryout. Her front teeth stuck out. In slacks and a loose shirt, her curvy body seemed merely stocky, and her bleached yellow curls, pinned carelessly on top of her head, looked messy.

But she had—what was it Clement had said?—she had a luster. Her own luscious aura shone from her.

"Everybody here?" Mr. Ettl asked.

Ted nodded.

"Then let's get started." Mr. Ettl ground out his cigarette on the floor with his heel. He shut his eyes and thrust his head forward from his heavy shoulders. "Imagine a summer Saturday in Paris. The sun is shining. We're on one of the grandest avenues in the world, the Champs-Élysées."

The name was only vaguely familiar to Fitzi. She memorized his pronunciation—*Shonz-elly-say*—in case it turned up in the reading.

"The avenue is crowded with tourists, promenading lovers, and—I know you're waiting for this—with *kids,*" Mr. Ettl went on. "The Louvre Museum is in the background. Gardens are on stage right. There's a carousel, a Punch and Judy show. A couple of mimes are doing their act."

Fitzi's parents! She glanced at Mom, who nodded and smiled encouragingly.

Mr. Ettl continued. "Can you see it? The curtain rising, the crowd scene?"

"Yes," whispered Fitzi and several of the others.

"When the curtain goes up, the overture is still playing. You can count on applause here."

Fitzi could almost hear it.

"The opening number starts right away: 'It's a beautiful day . . . on the Champs-Élysées . . . Where anything can happen . . . anything can happen . . .' " Though he only crooned, the joy and jump of the song got across to them. Some of the kids swayed lightly. The director snapped his fingers, an underbeat to his description. "There's color, music, movement. Paris is celebrating summer before our eyes!"

A young kid did a short tap step, then stopped, looking embarrassed.

"That's okay, son, I'm as excited as you are."

Everybody laughed.

"Okay. Then the stage revolves. Scene Two. Completely different set. Different mood. Now we're in a French country town. Nothing going on. Six kids wander onstage. Believe me, they are *bored*. They wish they could get out of this town and go to—three guesses."

"Paris!" a girl piped.

"You got it." Mr. Ettl laughed. "Then, very wistfully— completely different mood, remember—the kids sing, 'It's a beautiful day on the Champs-Élysées.' One of them—a teenage boy named Claude—turns upstage and notices something none of them clued into before. There's a collapsed *hot-air balloon* in a *tree*. Everybody know what a hot-air balloon looks like?"

Tiffany answered immediately, "Like a huge colored parachute with a basket hanging from it."

"That's right. The gondola—that's the basket—is what people ride in, and it's empty. Somebody's made an emergency landing, and disappeared." He paused. "So the kids have a terrific idea. They'll steal the balloon and go to Paris!"

"Right on!" somebody murmured.

"The stage revolves again." Mr. Ettl's fingers spun. "We're back in Paris. Now, kids, I want you to pay attention to this part."

They were already hanging on every word.

"The first act ends with the most spectacular entrance ever seen on Broadway. The Parisians are still milling around. One girl—her name's Gaby—looks up at the sky." He pointed up. Enthralled, Fitzi held her breath.

"Everybody else looks, too. Then Gaby shouts, 'Anything can happen on the Champs-Élysées!' and the balloon appears in the sky. The six country kids are in the gondola. The balloon floats down and lands onstage! How do you like *that?*"

Cheers.

"The two biggest parts are Gaby and Claude," Mr. Ettl explained. "One young schoolboy named Pierre has a lot to do, too. Those of you who aren't quite right for leads will have a chance at smaller roles. Or you may be picked as standbys. The rest will be in the chorus."

Fitzi saw the relief on several mothers' faces, including her own mom's. One way or another, every kid here would be in the show. With a sudden sense of companionship, the kids exchanged quick smiles and edged closer together.

The director said, "We won't use accents. Since the whole cast is supposed to be French, the audience will just go along with the assumption that they're speaking French. Clear?"

Distressed, one girl said, "I worked up a really good French accent."

"Sorry about that," Mr. Ettl told her coolly. "If there are no questions, let's get started."

His assistant, Ted, spoke for the first time. "Before we go any further, is anybody scared of the idea of riding down in the balloon?"

Fitzi's heart blipped in her throat.

Ted went on, "It won't be falling free, but it *will* start high. You'll have to take an elevator to the second floor of the theater to get into it."

"Does Gaby ever go in the balloon?" one of the girls asked timidly.

"No."

Nobody else said anything.

"Okay, Ted, it's all yours." Mr. Ettl withdrew to the side of the room and sat down to watch and listen.

Consulting his list, Ted asked Mark and Tiffany to stay where they were. Everybody else was to sit quietly on the floor, out of the way, while the two read.

Fitzi was glad she didn't have to read first, since nobody had ever seen the script before. It was easy to bungle a cold reading.

"Let's begin with Gaby's line, 'Anything can happen on the Champs-Élysées,' " Ted suggested. "In the next scene, the balloon is down, Claude climbs out, and they get acquainted. Read right on into that scene. Ready?"

Tiffany and Mark both nodded. Tiffany looked pale; not only did she have to read first, she also had to begin with an important line. Fitzi knew that was hard.

There was a short silence. Tiffany suddenly looked up. She seemed electrified. The wonder in her eyes almost created a giant balloon, floating slowly down. She shook her head incredulously. "Anything—" she said slowly, as though astonished, "*anything* can happen on the Champs-Élysées!"

She was so convincing that half the people in the room were still looking at the ceiling when she finished the line.

SEVEN

Tiffany was cast in the important role of Gaby; Mark was Claude. The earnest little kid, whose real name was Bernie, won the part of Pierre.

Fitzi was chosen as Tiffany's understudy, her standby. She would also have a solo dance number in the third act. She was happy with her assignments, and profoundly relieved. She wouldn't have to float down in the balloon, sing, or even stay long in the spotlight, yet she was *in the show*. On Broadway. With Mark Hiller.

As soon as the cast was announced, the papers ran pictures and stories about the leads, Monique Ormelle and

Burt Janus. Tiffany and Mark, the kids with the biggest parts, suddenly had news value, too. Several articles about them rushed into print.

At this, Fitzi felt a pang of envy. If she had been cast as Gaby, she would be the one tied to Mark, in the papers and maybe in his mind.

Tiffany was quoted as saying she must have been born under a lucky star. Asked if she had expected to win her role over so many contenders, she answered cryptically, "I believe in fate."

Mark, leaving his long stint on the soap opera *The Inner Tempest,* explained, "My contract's up for renewal this fall, and I won't sign on again. Hate to say good-bye to that great cast—we're like a family"—reading this, Fitzi could imagine his charming smile—"but the role in *Crowd Scene* is a major opportunity."

Fitzi wondered if she could ever sound as cool and smooth as those two.

Crowd Scene's PR man learned of the relationship between Clement Dale and the Wolpers. He set up a publicity interview with the four of them. Soon their pictures, too, were in the paper, under the heading, SHOW BUSINESS FAMILY FEATURED IN FORTHCOMING BROADWAY PRODUCTION.

Questioned by reporters, Clement proclaimed, "The performing tradition runs deep among us."

Mom and Dad, identified as the mimes "lately starring in the off-Broadway hit *Visions,*" told of "giving our lives to the theater."

Fitzi offered, "It's an honor to be in this show."

The morning the interview was published, Mark called. Fitzi recognized his voice even before he said who it was. Feeling strangled, she tried to be casual: "Oh. Hi."

"I saw the story about you and your family. It was impressive."

"Impressive? Us?" She hated herself for sounding so naive. "Oh, *impressive,*" she repeated, as if she hadn't heard him right the first time. "Thanks."

"I didn't know your grandfather was Clement Dale."

"Oh, no? I mean, oh, *yes.*" What was wrong with her? She bit her tongue and managed an airy laugh. "He is."

"Clement Dale was one of my idols when I was a little kid. I watched him every day on TV. He played The Singing Clock on *Junior Matinee.*"

Mark's warm voice could create a mood, even on the phone; as he described his enchantment with The Singing Clock, Fitzi remembered her grandfather going "Bing-Bong" so buoyantly. "He was wonderful."

"He was," Fitzi agreed.

"Well, it's something special for me. Working with Clement Dale and his family."

Fitzi responded in a rush, "I feel that way about working with you." Then second thoughts flooded in, and she wished she had been more restrained.

"I'll see you at rehearsal, then."

"Yes." She added formally, "Thank you for calling."

That afternoon, she waited impatiently for *The Inner*

Tempest to come on. She hadn't seen it for a long while, and wasn't sure if Mark's story line was still going.

His taped image appeared on the screen. He looked different from the way he did in real life. On the tube, he had puffy blow-dried hair, hip clothes, a jittery laugh. The character he played was reckless and wild; not like the person she knew.

His smile was the same, though. Fitzi stared into his eyes, brown, flecked with gold, as the camera zoomed in for a closeup. She knew she would never be able to look into somebody's eyes like this if he were here in the flesh.

But she pretended he was, and that they knew each other better, and she was not shy.

"I like you," she whispered to the taped image; and realized it didn't describe how she felt.

Now she wished she had been bolder on the phone. She turned off the TV and pondered the situation, then grabbed the phone book and flipped through to Hiller. There were a lot of them—no Mark—and she didn't know where he lived or what his father's first name was.

She did know that *The Inner Tempest* was taped in a studio in the fifties, and he had been working there for years. It made sense to assume he lived nearby. She checked the listings again, and found three in that area.

Impulsively she dialed one of those numbers. It didn't answer.

The second was busy.

Her fingers were shaking as she dialed the third. Mark answered. "Hello?"

"Oh, hi. Hi." Fitzi knew she sounded madly flustered. She regretted her impulsiveness, and nearly hung up; probably would have, but was afraid he had recognized her voice. Retreating into formality again, she said, "This is Fitzi Wolper. We spoke earlier."

To her surprise, he seemed pleased. "Yes, Fitzi. Hello again."

"I just happened to think—I have some old videos of *Junior Matinee*. With my grandfather. I didn't know if you'd like to see them, probably not, but—"

His voice lifted. "I'd love to."

"Well, we have them," Fitzi wandered on haplessly. "I mean, they're here—so is he," she added, on inspiration. "My grandfather, I mean. I'm sure he'd enjoy showing them to us." She hoped this was true; Clement could be so temperamental. Still, he liked to reminisce about the old days.

"Could I come now, then?" Mark asked.

"Sure." Fitzi could hardly believe this. "Yes," she added joyfully, and gave him the address.

"I'll be there in about half an hour, if that's okay."

"Oh, it is. Yes. It's fine." Suffused with happiness, Fitzi set down the phone and sat stunned for a moment. Then she raced out to the living room and yelled, "Clement! Guess what!"

Her grandfather bounded out of his room, his pointed eyebrows raised. "The building's on fire."

"Mark's coming over. He wants to see our old *Junior Matinee* tapes. He's a big fan of yours."

"Ah." Her grandfather beamed, gratified. "Mutual admiration. He's a talented fellow."

In an unaccustomed fit of housekeeping, Fitzi dashed around the living room, folding scattered newspapers and plumping cushions. She changed from jeans to a yellow jumpsuit, fluffed her hair.

Mark arrived promptly. Clement let him in, saying cordially, "I hear you're partial to old videos."

"I'd certainly like to see yours, sir."

Still in her room, hairbrush in hand, Fitzi listened, swallowing. She felt suddenly strangled with shyness. While Clement and Mark chatted, she drew long slow breaths, visualizing an egg. Finally she was calm enough to go out to the living room.

Mark looked taller than ever in the small room, and his smile seemed to light up every corner. "Hello, Fitzi."

Her shyness melted. She smiled back at him.

"How about diet sodas all round?" Clement suggested. "Then we can settle down in comfort. Fitzi?"

"Yes, please."

Sounds good," Mark agreed.

They relaxed on the large sofa in front of the VCR, and Clement started a tape. The Singing Clock appeared, tolling out the guest stars that would appear on the day's show.

"I remember this one!" Mark exclaimed. He put on glasses, which Fitzi had never seen him wear before. The heavy rims made him look different, studious.

Most of the show featured its regulars. Then the music and comedy star Victor Borge appeared on the screen.

While he played a classical piano piece, Chopin's rapid *Minute Waltz,* The Singing Clock chanted, "Ticketytockety, there goes a minute—"

No matter how fast Borge played, the clock kept just ahead of him. The pianist rattled through the waltz again, and then again, faster each time; and each time, the Clock sang faster still. The pianist's comic frustration, mounting to hysteria, was marvelous to see.

So was the deadpan precision of the unfeeling Clock. Fitzi and Mark laughed till they were gasping for breath. At the final "Bing-Bong" from the clock that signaled the end of the show, they both turned to Clement and applauded vigorously.

He made a small courtly bow.

As he left, Mark said, "This has meant a lot to me, Mr. Dale."

"Very kind, very kind." Clement thanked him graciously.

After Mark had gone, Fitzi and her grandfather stayed on in the living room, drinking another soda, caught in the spell of the long-ago show.

Fitzi realized something about herself that she had never known before. She said, "I'd like to be remembered for something really good I've done."

Her grandfather nodded. "It's a fine feeling. You don't need a long part to capture an audience. Bewitch them for three minutes, and they'll remember you forever."

EIGHT

"I hope you're not too upset." It was Tiffany on the phone, in one of her poison-sweet moods. They hadn't talked in the week since the Gaby role was cast.

Fitzi's temper leaped to the challenge. "Upset? About what?"

"Losing. Well, not *losing* exactly, but coming in second."

"You mean because I can fool around backstage every night while you get thrown to the wolves? No, I'm not upset."

"You actually gave a very good interpretation. It's nothing to be disappointed about."

"Which is probably why I'm not."

"Anyway." Tiffany's confident tone faltered. "I was wondering if you and I could go over our lines together. We both have to learn the part, and it's *long*. Have you gotten your sides yet?"

"Yes. It *is* long. And then there are the songs and dances. And of course," Fitzi added importantly, "I have a separate dance of my own in Act Three."

"For Gaby, we could take turns cueing each other."

Fitzi sensed a seeking for something—support, praise—from Tiffany's end of the line. Her irritation evaporated. "Okay, sure."

"We could talk over the interpretation," Tiffany said with quick intensity. "I could come to your place. Or we can meet wherever you want."

"We'll work out something."

"This is my big chance, you know?"

Alerted by her fervor, Fitzi replied, "Well, that's right. And everybody's got—you know, faith in you. Mr. Ettl and the rest of them."

"Not necessarily. Even if I was the best, it doesn't mean I'm any good."

Thanks a lot, Fitzi thought. "Trust me. You'll be sensational."

·

Fitzi and Pip were in the kitchen of Karen's apartment, helping her bake cookies. Karen had bought her mom a cat-shaped cookie jar for her birthday—Mrs. Edman was crazy about cookies and also about cats—and wanted to present it full of fresh-baked treats. Her mom would be out till six, so this was a perfect opportunity.

"Memorizing and rehearsing Gaby will be tough, but at least I'll never have to perform it." Fitzi popped a walnut in her mouth.

"How do you know?" Karen asked. "Tiffany might get sick."

"Never," Fitzi declared. "She'd die before she'd let anybody go on for her."

"But don't you mind that?" Pip stirred chocolate chips into the batter. "You'll have to be at the theater every night, just doing nothing. Standing by until Act Three."

"But I'll *be* there. I'll be on salary, watching my whole family perform. And I can get a lot of studying done and keep up to grade level."

"Well, that's good. Otherwise us junior high people might get ahead of you," Pip grinned.

"Anyway, I do have the solo dance."

"What happens if *you* get sick?" Pip asked.

"A kid in the chorus takes it."

"Like musical chairs."

"Yeah."

"Think we should have bought butterscotch chips, too?" Karen asked. A frown puckered her freckled forehead. "For variety?"

"Not really," Fitzi said. "Nothing beats chocolate. And we've got the mini-marshmallows for the coconut balls." With a fine surge of well-being, she stirred and greased and tasted until it was time to go home for supper.

Then she walked the two blocks slowly, enjoying pleasant drifting images of the neighborhood around her. She was aware of good smells from the delis and restaurants; of rangy geraniums in apartment windows, their stems pressed against the safety grilles; of late-afternoon sun between tall buildings. The dense, sultry August day was shifting toward evening, and like Fitzi, a lot of people were hurrying home.

·

"Evening, my beauty," Lance Harrington greeted Fitzi, as she answered the door. His false teeth gleamed like even little pebbles.

"Don't hang there in the doorway, come in, come in," Clement called curtly from his room. The two men were going to cue each other on their lines.

Fitzi's grandfather was in a terrible mood. Last year, right after his stroke, his memory had been poor, and he still worried about it. With rehearsals starting next week, he claimed his lines wouldn't stick in his head, his brain had turned to mush, he wished he had never gotten the part of Bistro Beau, and everybody might as well face the fact, right now, that it was going to be a catastrophe. None of the family paid much attention to this, since he seemed able to rattle the lines off perfectly.

Mom rolled her eyes in silent exasperation toward his room, and smiled at Lance. "Have you eaten yet? Want a sandwich?"

"No, thank you, I'm fine. I'll go join the lion in his den."

As the week passed, Lance and Clement tossed lines at

each other until Fitzi figured she could stand by for either one of them. Meanwhile Dad spent hours and hours teaching Mom to juggle. He was a skilled juggler, but she could barely keep three oranges in the air.

"I'll never get it!" she cried wildly one evening, as an orange rolled under the sofa, far out of reach. She burst into tears. Sobbing, she flung herself on the exercise mat they kept by the window.

"Now, sweetheart, that was almost perfect," Dad soothed. He pulled a mock-serious face. "Just your bad luck you got a runaway orange."

"It's not *funny!* I'll probably be *fired!*"

Dad smoothed the black points of hair on her forehead, murmuring, "We'll keep working till you get it."

"And I'm no good at the magic tricks either! Fitzi said she can always figure out what I'm doing!"

Dad looked at Fitzi reproachfully.

Fitzi spread her hands, helpless. "I always can."

The phone rang. Fitzi answered it. It was Tiffany. She wanted to come to the Wolpers' and go over lines tonight.

"I'll call you back," Fitzi told her cautiously.

She broached the idea to her parents. Dad protested, "Tonight? Now?"

"That's what she said."

"It'll be eight o'clock before she even gets here," he pointed out. Tiffany lived downtown and would have to take the bus.

Dad sighed, his narrow face annoyed. "I really don't

want to go out tonight at ten or eleven o'clock and take her home. Can somebody come for her?"

Fitzi shook her head.

"How about her father?"

"Her parents are divorced. Her father lives in San Diego, Dad. And her mom just got in from work."

Mom grumbled, "That kid's always wandering around on her own. Acrobatics class, auditions, there's never anybody with her." Since Tiffany had gotten the role of Gaby, and Fitzi was only her standby, Mom found fault wherever she could.

"Not everybody my age gets supervised like a baby," Fitzi retorted. Actually, she didn't mind having adult company, especially at night. Tiffany had been robbed of her change purse twice, and now routinely carried her fare in her shoe. "Anyway, what'll I tell her?"

"Tell her we're sorry, but not tonight, babe. Tomorrow afternoon would be okay," Dad said. He and Mom started with the oranges again.

Fitzi called Tiffany, then shut herself in her room and took out her notebook. She looked through some of the entries she had made in it during the past year—notes about her life, stories she had written, bits from her horoscope. She and Karen were both Libras; occasionally they tried to keep track of whether the newspaper prophecies came true.

It was hard to tell. "New influences cause conflict." That had been a couple of months ago. "Romantic pressures build." And the last, "You will find that certain someone."

She closed the notebook and lay on her bed, a little sleepy, daydreaming.

Around her, the shell pink walls of her room were veiled with shadows. She imagined herself moving through them, finding someone . . . finding Mark.

NINE

The character of Gaby was supposed to be a rags-and-tatters Parisian girl with a hard-knock life. Next afternoon at the Wolpers', it bothered Tiffany when she and Fitzi read it two different ways.

"You sound so wistful," Tiffany complained, as they took turns cueing each other.

"I see her like that," Fitzi said stubbornly.

"I'm going for a real gutsy impression."

"Do what you want. We're just practicing lines, anyway."

"She should be strong, in my opinion. You're making her wimpy."

"Look, do you want to quit for today? You know the lines anyway."

"No, let's go on."

An hour later, bored to death and sick of *Crowd Scene,* Fitzi rebelled. "Tiffany, we're stopping. *Now.*"

"We can't," Tiffany insisted stubbornly. "I've got to go over that last scene once more."

"*Why?* You've got it down cold. And I'm famished. My folks ate dinner half an hour ago."

"I *hesitated* over one line. I can't hesitate."

"So spit it right out next time," Fitzi told her adamantly. She threw down the script and marched out of her room. Tiffany followed reluctantly.

In the living room, Mom was juggling onions while Dad watched. "A little higher, a little higher," he urged her. "Let's let the audience see them."

"Whenever I get the rhythm right, you throw me off!" Mom cried, barely keeping the onions aloft, arms flailing.

"Doing fine, doing fine," Dad said.

From Clement's room, Lance declaimed, "So, Bistro Beau! A group of children have captured your heart!"

Fitzi's grandfather responded: "Not my heart, only my wallet! I've been robbed!"

Fitzi mumbled the words of the play along with him, adding irritably, "I hate to break in, but is there anything to eat?"

"No, we decided to starve you today," Dad told her, his eyes on Mom's juggling.

"Unless you want onions." Mom kept them flying as she spoke. Her upper lip was beaded with sweat. It was a hot August day, and the apartment wasn't air-conditioned.

Fitzi sighed. "Are you pushing anything in particular?"

"There's Japanese takeout in the fridge. Plenty for you, too, Tiffany," Dad said.

Fitzi put the cartons of food on the table. She told Tiffany ungraciously, "I hope you don't want anything heated."

"Oh, no."

Fitzi sat down and started eating.

"I can eat later, at home," Tiffany offered, with token politeness. But when Fitzi shoved a plate in front of her, she took a seat, and helped herself to cold fish and rice.

In the other room, Lance and Clement started the pickpocket scene again. Mom kept juggling. The girls ate steadily.

"It must be weird, having your parents in the same show," Tiffany commented in an undertone. "*And* your grandfather."

"Everything's weird. Our whole family's weird. You're weird yourself," Fitzi threw out, still in a temper.

Tiffany put her fork down. "I could go home," she said unhappily. Her wide face, with the pointy front teeth, was dismayed.

Fitzi said quickly, "I didn't mean it like that. It's only—" Karen and Pip flashed into her mind, busy with projects, easy to be with, never taxing themselves much. While she and Tiffany sweated and worried and tried to be the *best*, the *best*, always the *best*, Karen and Pip went shopping, took in a movie—they were free to have fun, ordinary easy fun. The sushi salty in her throat, Fitzi envied them.

"Only what?" Tiffany asked.

"Oh . . . if we're uptight now, what'll we be during rehearsals?"

"Worse," Tiffany prophesied. "And on opening night, the worst of all." She added pensively, "I wonder if my dad'll come. I guess not."

"Why not?"

"He's furious about me being in the show."

Fitzi looked at her, amazed. She had never heard of a parent feeling like that. *"Why?"*

"Oh, you know how he and my mom are. They're always trying to spite each other."

Fitzi did know. She remembered when the Resnicks were divorced, a couple of years ago. They had fought bitterly for custody of Tiffany. Even now, they continued to quarrel over visitation rights. Tiffany even hated to tell either parent what the other had said on the phone; it always seemed to be cause for a blowup.

"But what does the show have to do with anything?" Fitzi asked.

"My dad's taking a vacation in Mexico in November, and the two of us were planning to go together. He blames Mom for getting me tied up so I can't go." She added gloomily, "They both seem to think everything in my life is designed to cause grief to them personally."

Fitzi nodded. Mexico. A vacation. In her present mood, it sounded irresistible. She asked curiously, "If you had the choice, which would you choose? The show or the trip?"

Tiffany answered indignantly, "I *did* have the choice. Mom doesn't make me audition, she's got a good job of her own."

"So you don't have any regrets."

"Oh, well, regrets. That's different," Tiffany said wryly. "I guess no matter what you decide, you're sort of sorry. . . . Anyway, I doubt if my dad'll come to opening night."

•

On the first day of rehearsal, Clement Dale and the three Wolpers waited outside their apartment building. They had arranged for a limo to pick up the four of them, each rehearsal morning. They all agreed it was worth anything to get to the theater on time and fresh, without the hassle of subway or bus.

Fitzi knew Tiffany's mother had made the same arrangement for her; probably a lot of cast members had. Still, as she saw commuters rushing to work, she had a sense of being extra lucky.

The car drove up, long and gray and impressive, just as it started to rain. Fitzi and her family exchanged swift smiles. They climbed into leather-scented luxury as the first drops fell.

Rehearsals weren't held where they had tried out, but in the theater where the show would actually open and play. It was gigantic, with almost two thousand seats. The stage was large enough to accommodate the hot-air balloon and the elaborate sets. Since these weren't there yet, the stage looked incredibly huge. Yet as the cast arrived and milled around, Fitzi could see how the space would fill up.

Everybody signed in with Duke, the security guard at the stage door. Duke was young; short and husky in his green uniform, with an amiable moon face. He seemed very anxious to do his job right, doublechecking the addresses and phone numbers on his cast list. He pleased Tiffany by telling her, "I read about you. You're sort of a star, right?"

His conscientiousness made the sign-in slow. Clement remarked to Lance, "Duke probably wants to break into show business."

Lance laughed, nodding. "Right. He hopes Seymour Ettl will notice him."

Her grandfather explained to Fitzi, "When Lance and I were young and starting out, the smart move was to get a job waiting tables at Sardi's. That's where the producers and directors hung out."

"Then you tried to make them notice you." Lance chuckled. "Your grandfather and I were the best darn waiters Sardi's ever had."

"*Did* anybody notice?" Fitzi asked.

"Never." Clement's eyes twinkled.

"Oh, we got a lot of good tips," Lance said. "But our show biz potential went unappreciated, alas."

Mr. Ettl wasn't paying any attention to Duke, either. He and Ted were talking to the rehearsal pianist.

When the cast finally assembled onstage, Fitzi recognized the stars, Burt Janus and Monique Ormelle. Burt Janus looked just like his photos, a barrel-shaped man with a comically oversized nose and carroty hair. Monique Ormelle was small and slight; without makeup, she seemed disappointingly plain. Her big eyes and high cheekbones, so striking in glamor shots, looked just ordinary, but she had a nice smile.

Mr. Ettl gave them a welcome and a pep talk: "When I look at you folks, I see talent. I see success. Most of all, I see a show where every role was carefully cast."

He went on, "Believe me, we had to make some hard choices. You're all so good—" He lifted his arms and dropped them helplessly, shaking his heavy head. "Hard choices," he repeated. "But now I'm convinced that you— *you,* each one of you—is exactly right for the part you've earned."

Thinking of her third act dance, Fitzi felt an inner chord of agreement. She could do that dance better than anybody. She was sure of it.

Mr. Ettl continued, "A few of you may be disappointed that you don't have bigger parts. If anybody feels that way, let me tell you, performing a small part brilliantly is better than being so-so in the lead. It does more for the part, more for the show, and more for you."

His eyes bored into their faces; Fitzi believed him. Her grandfather had said the same thing.

"So, everybody, please give it all you've got. Let's have a smash hit!" the director ended, raising his fists in a gesture of triumph.

The cast applauded.

They set to work. Mr. Ettl broke people into groups and described, in general, how he wanted them to block in their moves. Ted started teaching the kids their songs and dances.

Fitzi soon realized that although standbys needed to know their parts just as thoroughly as the principals did, it was really the principals who rehearsed, while the understudies watched. She scarcely dared blink for fear she would miss something. For most of the day, she and Jerry Dominic, Mark's standby, stood together, their eyes locked on Tiffany and Mark as if life depended on it.

There were long stretches when Monique Ormelle and Burt Janus, and other adults, worked out scenes that had no kids in them. During these periods, Mr. Ettl made it clear that they were to remain quiet and still. Ted hushed anybody who uttered so much as a whisper.

Nobody was expected to be word-perfect in lines at the beginning, but every slip-up brought an immediate fear: *Will they be sorry they picked me?*

Fitzi knew nearly every kid in the show felt that way. So did her parents, when they made mistakes in their routine. So did her grandfather and Lance, though they were quick about blocking their stage moves and could hum songs almost as soon as they heard them. And, like Tiffany, they knew their lines perfectly.

For most of that first hectic day, Fitzi and Mark barely exchanged a word. But during the afternoon break, everybody could relax and talk.

She saw Mark sitting on the side, listening to Clement and Lance reminisce. The two old men were talking about long-ago shows in other huge theaters.

"Remember when Houdini made an elephant disappear from the stage of the Hippodrome?" Lance chuckled.

"Ah, Houdini! One of the best magicians who ever lived," Fitzi's grandfather answered.

Mom, wearily practicing a disappearing flower trick nearby, asked, "Where is he now, when we need him?"

Fitzi sank into an empty chair beside Mark. He smiled at her, the warmth in his eyes drawing her in. She felt like leaning against him, maybe simply collapsing.

She turned stiffly away, and watched her father stroll by, followed by a couple of little kids. He was showing them the mime puppet walk.

Mark asked her gently, "How's it going?"

Fitzi wanted to say something clever. Instead she spoke the truth: "I can't figure out what Tiffany's doing in that last number. When I try crossing behind the line, I get out of step. I don't know if I should ask Ted or Tiffany, they've both got plenty of problems—"

Mark stood up. "You have to start counting on the downbeat . . . *and three, and four* . . . come on, try it with me."

As they tapped and counted, the pattern grew clear to Fitzi. She brushed wisps of dark hair out of her eyes. "Thank you," she said after a minute. They sat down.

He shrugged, dismissing the need for thanks. "I have trouble, too. This isn't a whole lot like a TV soap."

"No." She grinned. "You've got more to worry about than I do, anyway. Tiffany's pretty healthy."

He nodded and laughed. He glanced over at Tiffany, who was practicing some tricky twirls. Somehow, even in rehearsal clothes, she had the right look for Gaby—a lush, unkempt appeal.

As Mark watched her, Fitzi felt a stab of jealousy. It didn't seem fair that some girls seemed to have a magnet inside them, while others—like Fitzi herself—simply looked interesting. If that.

Ted, shouted, "Okay, everybody, let's get back to it. Standbys over here. Please pay attention."

They never got to Fitzi's third act dance that afternoon, and she was glad. By the time the cast was finally dismissed, she was frazzled and worn out. Because rehearsals would end at different times each day—whenever Mr. Ettl let them go—no car would be meeting them. It was off to the subway, in the rush hour, in the rain.

TEN

With rehearsals underway, the summer seemed to accelerate. It moved too fast. There was too much to do, too much to learn, too much to get used to. A small crowd of fans gathered each day at the stage door. Reporters turned up to get—or invent—human interest stories about Janus and Ormelle, and about the kids who were in the show with them. Suddenly they were all celebrities.

Tensions broke out backstage. Jerry Dominic, Mark's standby, kept moaning, "Boy, am I confused." One morning Mark snapped at him, "Study the script, for Pete's sake! That's the third time you've asked me about a line!"

Lance kept crossing the stage in the wrong place during one of Clement's songs. Finally Clement retaliated by tripping him with his cane.

As August slid into September, some of the young cast members went to professional children's classes. Others were privately tutored. Fitzi's parents arranged for a tutor to come to their apartment every other weekday evening. For a couple of hours, Mr. Nilson crammed knowledge into Fitzi. On alternate nights, she did homework.

It wasn't ideal—nothing really could be—but she was a quick study, used to racing through schoolwork whenever it could be fitted in. Once the show opened, Mr. Nilson would tutor her at the theater; probably during Acts One and Two, when she was merely standing by.

.

The Saturday before school started, Karen gave a party for some of the old P.S. 166 crowd. Fitzi went, just for an hour, but felt out of place. Although she was glad to see the kids she had gone to school with, she thought they treated her differently. Some seemed overly impressed by her new life. Others assumed she had gotten stuck-up, and snubbed or ignored her. She wasn't really one of them anymore.

Still, Karen was careful to ask, "When's your show opening?"

"Early December."

"Well, my folks and I'll be there," Karen promised. "Pip, too."

Fitzi reminded herself that these were her best friends.

Warmed, she said, "It wouldn't be the same without you."

The day school began, Fitzi and her family were getting into the limo just as Pip hurried off to classes. She was wearing a new fall jacket. She had had her hair cut; the long fair braid was replaced by a short permanent. It made her look older.

"Hi!" the girls greeted each other briefly, and went their separate ways.

.

As word continued to flow out through the media about *Crowd Scene,* Tiffany and Mark especially caught the public's interest. They were in constant demand for public appearances. Pictures and articles about them were featured in newspapers and magazines.

Fitzi watched them together wistfully. She kept wishing Mark were with her instead.

The small crowd grew ever larger by the stage door, waiting for rehearsals to break each day. Most of these people would wait around just once, get autographs, and then be off to some other stage door, never to be seen again. But a few were repeaters.

One burly man was there almost every afternoon. He stood in the gathering on the sidewalk, his dirty clothes tied around his waist with a rope, his eyes fixed on the door until Tiffany came through it. Then he always stepped forward slightly, as though ready to tear the whole world apart. When people approached Tiffany, he glared until they moved away.

One day as Fitzi and her parents left by the stage door,

Tiffany was just ahead of them, bedraggled and exhausted. She paused, confronted by a small circle of waiting fans. A woman recognized her, and asked for her autograph.

In an instant, Tiffany was transformed. Her face lit up like a beacon. Head high, wreathed in charm, she bustled forward, her laughter pulling all eyes toward her. She signed her name on the scrap of paper the woman held.

"Oh, thank you." The woman edged away, as if from royalty.

Tiffany turned to Fitzi. "It's beginning," she murmured joyfully.

Fitzi, feeling like a wrinkled rag and thankful to be unnoticed, answered, "Better you than me."

Two teenage girls rushed forward. Neither held pens or paper. Instead, one pulled a bobby pin roughly from Tiffany's blonde curls, yanking her hair in the process.

Startled, Tiffany shrank back, her hand flying to her head.

The burly man lunged from the waiting circle of people on the sidewalk. He shoved the teenager away from Tiffany.

"Don't touch her," he commanded hoarsely. His hair was an unruly mop, his eyes fierce. "I don't allow anybody to touch her."

Tiffany looked up at the man blankly.

The teenagers ran away.

Fitzi's grandfather stepped quickly to Tiffany's side and asked, "Headed for the bus? We'll walk with you."

Ringed by him and the three Wolpers, Tiffany hurried off.

Mrs. Resnick heard about this, and changed her work schedule. From then on, she arrived at the theater in the late afternoon, waited for rehearsal to end, and accompanied Tiffany home.

"It's silly," Tiffany told Fitzi. "He's just a fan. It's sort of exciting to be so much admired, don't you think?"

"No," Fitzi said honestly. "He looks a little off the wall to me. I'd be scared."

Tiffany laughed.

A week later, she confided to Fitzi, "Mom thinks she saw that man outside our apartment building."

"Doing what?"

"Just watching the building."

"Waiting for you?" Fitzi asked.

Tiffany preened, smiling her luscious smile. "I guess so. We don't know what he was doing, actually, but why else would he hang around?"

Mrs. Resnick pointed the man out to Duke, the young security guard at the stage door, and asked him to make sure the fan never got past him, into the theater. She told Fitzi's parents she wished they had a doorman at their apartment building.

•

Toward the end of September, *Crowd Scene*'s sets were built onstage, and the cast's problems redoubled. Now the blocking of moves had to be translated into places on revolving scenery, and, for a few people, inside the basket of a falling balloon.

The complicated sets didn't work right. Breakaway

buildings collided, platforms revolved in the wrong direction, the hot-air balloon refused to float down.

Mr. Ettl didn't even try to rehearse the balloon landing with kids in the basket. He kept them onstage while the crew wrestled with the lowering mechanism.

"When do you think they'll put us up there?" Bernie asked Mark apprehensively.

"Not until they're positive it's safe," Mark assured him.

On another morning, Bernie commented nervously, "If we were in that basket now, we'd be stranded at a very high level." The stage crew had tried—and failed, for the third time that day—to get the thing moving.

"We'd climb out onto the platform, and take the elevator down," Mark told him reasonably.

Bernie nodded, but didn't look altogether convinced.

Fitzi was grateful, again, that she never had to get into the balloon. It was hard enough just learning Gaby's entrances and exits, around the Paris buildings that had sprung up onstage.

Her third act dance, the one number she would actually perform before the audience, was changed, too. Now she had to tap up and down a flight of stairs. After a moment of fear on the top landing, she hurtled through the number with such style and abandon that even Mr. Ettl looked admiring.

"Spectacular, babe," Dad whispered, juggling past her.

Mark caught up with her long enough to praise her dance, and to add, "I'd like to come by and see you at home again, Fitzi, if we ever get a spare minute."

"I'd like that, too."

But spare minutes were hard to come by. Although there was a lot of waiting while Ormelle and Janus rehearsed scenes that had no kids in them, Mr. Ettl and Ted continued to enforce the rule of quiet, stillness, and general invisibility.

This sharpened Fitzi's concentration. She watched the evolving performances closely. She especially liked the duet Janus and Ormelle sang in Act Two, "This Will Never Be a Romance." She began to see the beauty Ormelle would project later, in makeup and costumes. Even with her hair pulled back and her face clean and shiny, Ormelle's voice and smile had a silvery magic.

In this duet, the chunky, homely man and glamorous woman admitted that they were drawn to each other, yet denied the attraction. Fitzi found this fascinating.

∙

Mr. Ettl kept them later and later, lunch breaks were shorter, everybody was jumpy and tired. By late afternoon on rehearsal days, Fitzi yearned only for dinner and bed.

Yet even on the longest days, their fans were faithful. At about six o'clock one night, with the rehearsal still in progress, there was a commotion at the stage door. Fitzi and a few other standbys edged over to see what was going on.

Duke, the security guard, was wrestling with Tiffany's burly fan. The disheveled man yelled incoherently, "It's too long—rehearsal's too long for Tiffany! No good for her! No good!"

Duke beeped for assistance, and two more security guards joined him from the back of the theater. They threw the fan out, and secured the theater.

"I really hate this job," Duke muttered, smoothing his hair.

Fitzi and the other standbys slipped back to their places. Onstage, Lance was proclaiming, "So, Bistro Beau! A group of children have captured your heart!"

Crossing the stage in pursuit of Tiffany, Clement roared, "Not my heart, only my wallet! I've been robbed!"

A few days later, Duke quit, and was replaced by an older guard named George.

.

Fitzi's birthday, October 4, was marked only by presents from her family and hasty cupcakes before bed. They had all spent a long day at rehearsal.

Pip didn't bring her a present this year. Fitzi saw her for a minute before supper. Pip swept into the apartment building with a group of junior high kids. They were all laughing and chattering. After a quick "hi" to Fitzi, she and her friends jammed into the rattly old elevator, leaving Fitzi and her family waiting for the next trip.

Pip had forgotten the date. Fitzi felt a sharp momentary hurt.

But Karen remembered—a couple of days late—and called with congratulations. They talked for a few minutes, a little awkwardly.

"Did you read our horoscope?" Karen asked.

"Gosh, no, I forgot." Between rehearsals and her hours

with the tutor, Fitzi never thought of horoscopes anymore. "Did you?"

"Yes. It was dull," Karen told her. "Domestic matters will rule, someone close to us will attain dominance, the usual stuff. Actually Scorpios have more exciting forecasts, have you noticed that?"

"Absolutely," Fitzi agreed eagerly. "We should have insisted on being born later." They both laughed. With an urge to reestablish their accord, Fitzi dragged out the discussion of horoscopes. Then she asked how school was going, and Karen asked how rehearsals were going.

On Karen's birthday a couple of weeks later, Fitzi called her in return, but she was out. Fitzi, with a muscle spasm in her leg and lessons still to do, couldn't help being glad she didn't have to talk about horoscopes again.

·

October, the golden month, had blown fresh excitement into the city. New shows had opened, new reviews were posted on theaters, new stars were born.

One Saturday night, with no rehearsal the next day, Fitzi and her family gave themselves a deserved treat. They cancelled Fitzi's tutoring session and ate dinner at Charlie O's, in Shubert Alley. Then they enjoyed a relaxed stroll around the theater district as the lights came on.

"We're part of this," Mom said, speaking like an enchanted child. "It's all ours." She and Dad hugged each other.

Later they all walked east, past Rockefeller Center, further to Madison, further to Park. Above the Pan Am building, an enormous harvest moon hung in the blue air like a giant pumpkin.

"There's no town like this," Clement said to Fitzi, his voice full of drama. "Never has been. Never will be."

Fitzi nodded, gazing at the sky. Even the moon put on a better show in New York.

E L E V E N

Fitzi stood in the wings with Jerry Dominic, waiting for the rehearsal to begin. They chatted with other standbys. Near them, Janus and Ormelle, the stars, were ready for their entrance cues.

Onstage, Fitzi's parents, her grandfather, Lance, and the whole chorus for the first number, stood around restlessly. It was November 2.

"Where's Tiffany?" Mr. Ettl asked Ted.

"She hasn't signed in yet," Ted told him.

Mr. Ettl sighed, his heavy shoulders bowed.

They waited a few minutes, not starting the rehearsal.

Mr. Ettl talked to one of the stagehands about the balloon, which still wasn't working right. Then he called to Ted, "Tiffany here yet?"

"Not yet, Seymour. She must be stuck in traffic."

"Okay. She's not in the country scene, let's run through that first. Sorry," he threw out with a placating smile to Janus and Ormelle, who weren't in it either.

Mark, Bernie, and four other kids gathered on the set that showed the dull country town. They ran through their version of "It's a Beautiful Day," discovered the crumpled balloon in a tree, and decided to fly to Paris.

At the end of this scene, Tiffany still hadn't shown up.

"Call her at home," Mr. Ettl told Ted.

He did, but nobody answered. "I tried her limo service, too," Ted reported. "They say the car went to pick her up this morning as usual, but she wasn't there."

Mr. Ettl asked, "They're certain?"

"Positive. The driver even went upstairs and knocked on the apartment door."

"And they haven't had a message from her? Or from Mrs. Resnick?"

"Not a word."

Like everybody else, Fitzi was puzzled. Tiffany had never missed a minute of rehearsal before.

"Fitzi, where are you?" the director called.

"Right here, Mr. Ettl, standing by."

"You'll have to fill in until she shows up."

"Yes, sir." Trying to appear calm and prepared, Fitzi stepped out of the wings.

The morning passed in a blur of nerves as she rehearsed the part of Gaby with the cast for the first time. She sensed that her family was equally nervous for her. Mom messed up the juggling more than ever. Dad, usually cool and professional under stress, fumbled his magic act. Only her grandfather, despite a net of tension around the eyes, carried off Bistro Beau with his customary flair.

Fitzi's chief problem was timing. Though she had learned Gaby's moves thoroughly, the chorus seemed to zoom through the dance numbers like fire through dry grass, while she struggled to catch them.

"Speed it up, Fitzi, speed it up," Ted kept yelling, above the rapid tinkle-tankle of the rehearsal piano. This just blew her concentration more. She went the wrong way in a stage cross and bumped into Monique Ormelle, got out of position in the Champs-Élysées number, hurt her neck in a series of head-snapping turns, and missed a music cue.

Mr. Ettl said wearily, "We'll have to go through that scene again."

Mortified, Fitzi saw Mark and little Bernie waiting to begin the second scene, on the next set. Mark's face was in shadow. She couldn't really see his eyes, but imagined his appraising gaze. *He's so good,* she grieved inwardly. *Everybody's better than me.*

The piano started again. She danced forward, smiling brightly. This time her pace was better, but her first song sounded thin and wistful in her own ears, nowhere near as effective as Tiffany's lusty rendition.

By the mid-morning break, she was ready to cry. Where could Tiffany be?

The cast scattered for the break. Fitzi's parents came toward her, gamely cheerful. Fitzi backed away from them. "I don't want to talk." She ran backstage and slipped outside to the alley behind the theater.

Cast members often came out here to get some air without having to face fans in the street. The alley was empty now, except for a familiar huddled figure in another doorway. Probably one of the city's homeless, the shapeless figure usually seemed to be around the theater someplace, barely noticed, like the shadows or the garbage cans.

Fitzi leaned against the side of the building, head bowed, letting the bad feelings drain out of her.

Somebody else came out of the theater. She turned quickly and saw Mark. "Oh—is it time for us to start again?"

"No, not quite," he answered.

"Has Tiffany come?"

"No. I'm just here, that's all." He moved beside her. Together they stood in silence in the smelly dank alley. Although they didn't speak or touch, Fitzi felt as if a current passed between them, linking them.

Most of her scenes were played with Mark after that, and everything went better for her. He prompted her under his breath whenever she faltered, guided her unobtrusively into position during the dances, and murmured encouragement before every song.

As they got to the third act, she saw her understudy for

the specialty dance—Alix Ashton, from the chorus—practically salivating at the chance to perform the number.

Sure enough, Mr. Ettl said, "Alix, take over Fitzi's dance today."

Fitzi watched rebelliously as Alix usurped her part. Fitzi had been chosen, over everybody else, to do this dance. It was *hers*. She knew exactly how it should be done, and she felt Alix was making a mess of it. Where was the flair, the precision, the breathtaking descent on the flight of stairs? Alix practically *clumped* down. She showed no grace at all.

Fitzi whispered scornfully to Mark, "She moves like a pudding."

Mark retained the interested face of a person new to Paris, and didn't answer.

Looking pleased with herself, Alix finished the dance, and the cast continued through to the end of the act.

Then Mr. Ettl decided to go back to Act One, where there were problems with the set. The hot-air balloon still wasn't working right; so far, nobody had ridden in it. Whenever they went over the scene where the country kids were supposed to drop down from the sky, Ted simply had them walk onstage, while the balloon lurched down jerkily, empty.

This time, though, the stage crew finally got it to float to the stage without a hitch. Mr. Ettl decided the six young actors should start getting used to riding in it. He told Ted to take them up to the second floor in the elevator; they would run through the scene properly.

To Fitzi, this was a welcome diversion. She forgot her

own troubles as Ted rounded up Mark and Bernie and the others.

Bernie, the smallest actor slated for the balloon ride, suddenly looked ready to faint. "I can't," he announced emphatically, and sat on the floor.

Mr. Ettl held his head in his hands. "We don't have enough trouble?" he asked the fates.

"You have to," Ted told Bernie grimly.

Bernie began to cry.

"Get up!" Bernie's mother called from out front, no doubt fearing her son would be replaced.

"No," Bernie sobbed.

Mark squatted beside the younger boy and talked quietly to him.

"No," Bernie said again.

Mark talked some more. Finally Bernie hauled himself to his feet, snuffling. Mark took his hand. They followed Ted to the elevator.

A minute later, the six kids appeared on a railed catwalk over the stage. The cast watched as Ted helped them, one by one, into the basket of the balloon. Bernie's thin voice pierced the theater: "This is the worst day of my life."

"Okay, everybody else, places for the balloon entrance," Mr. Ettl commanded.

The piano player struck up his tune. Instantly, smiles streaked across the stage like rays of sun. The Paris scene sprang into life, its colorful crowd milling among the breakaway buildings. Mom juggled, Dad pulled a flower out of the air, Clement and Lance swung their walking sticks smartly.

Fitzi planted herself center stage, stared upward, and declared, "*Anything* can happen on the Champs-Élysées!"

And the balloon drifted down beautifully. It drifted until it was about fifteen feet off the ground. Then the lowering mechanism stuck. The balloon remained where it was, its basket swaying gently.

Until this point, Bernie, though green, had masked his fright with a ghastly grin. But, stuck in midair, he began to shriek.

His mother called from her seat, "Don't panic, Bernie!"

Ted, on the catwalk above, shouted directions to the stage crew.

In the balloon, Mark looked harried and exasperated.

In the midst of this uproar, Tiffany's mother entered the theater. She came onstage and grabbed Mr. Ettl's sleeve, forcing his attention.

"Please, Mrs. Resnick, we've got a crisis here," the director protested.

Mrs. Resnick explained that Ted had phoned her at work to see if she knew where Tiffany was. Until that moment—only about half an hour ago—she had assumed her daughter was at rehearsal.

"Where can she be?" she kept repeating.

"Mrs. Resnick, I understand your concern, but there's a rehearsal going on," Mr. Ettl said. "More or less," he added, glancing up at the stuck balloon.

"But my daughter's missing. She's *missing*."

"She'll turn up any minute," Mr. Ettl soothed. "In the meanwhile, Mrs. Resnick, please, off the stage."

Fitzi watched Tiffany's mom walk slowly down the side steps into the auditorium. She was a short, sturdy-boned woman, her wide face unseeing with distress. She sat out front. Slowly, she shredded a Kleenex in her hands.

Within a few minutes the stage crew had fixed the balloon mechanism. The basket glided onto the stage for a perfect landing. Bernie scrambled out, others followed.

Jumping into character, Mark climbed over the side and asked Fitzi charmingly, "Is this Paris?"

They continued with the dialogue of the next scene. It was the one Mr. Ettl had used in the tryouts, where Gaby and Claude question each other and get acquainted. As Fitzi spoke the lines, describing her character's tough life, she remembered how Tiffany always tossed them out boldly, with her own gutsy confidence. Now it seemed to her that her interpretation *did* sound wimpy, just as Tiffany had said.

Unnerved, she floundered in a long speech, losing track of where they were in the scene. Mark rescued her by ad-libbing until she started saying the right lines again.

"Okay, okay," Mr. Ettl groaned. "That's enough for today." He forced a smile. "Tomorrow's another day."

Fitzi and her family got their things and started out the stage door. It was raining heavily. No fans were waiting on the sidewalk, this awful afternoon.

Fitzi's grandfather paused to open his umbrella. Mrs.

Resnick caught up with them. She said urgently, "Fitzi, I need to talk to you."

"Okay," Fitzi answered helplessly, battered by spits of rain.

Dad tried to intervene. "Mrs. Resnick, I think we should all go home."

With an apologetic glance at him, Mrs. Resnick persisted. "Fitzi, you're Tiffany's friend. You'd know, if anybody would."

"Know what?"

"Was she upset about anything?"

Fitzi's tired brain was a blank. "I haven't seen her since yesterday."

"I *mean* yesterday."

A passing cab sped through a puddle, deluging them with muddy water. Wiping feebly at her warm-up pants, her face running with rain, Fitzi could barely remember yesterday.

Mrs. Resnick started another agitated plea. "How about that awful man? That crazy fan?"

Mom cut in, her voice warm and sympathetic. "Mrs. Resnick, I bet Tiffany's at home right now. There's probably been some kind of misunderstanding."

"A misunderstanding," Dad echoed eagerly. "Maybe she thought the rehearsal was called off and went shopping—or whatever. You know how kids are."

Mrs. Resnick hesitated, then nodded numbly.

Dad flagged down a cab. He helped Tiffany's mom into it, saying heartily, "Have a good dinner. We'll see you tomorrow—and Tiffany too, for sure."

TWELVE

When they got home, Dad called Mr. Nilson, Fitzi's tutor, to tell him not to come over tonight. He explained that Fitzi had had a hard day, and needed extra rest. Mr. Nilson understood. He taught several other show business kids.

Then Mom ordered takeout from U-Call Hot Plates, and Fitzi got to choose exactly what she wanted—a big chicken dinner with mashed potatoes, and a slice of apple pie. They all treated Tiffany's absence as one of those passing events that would soon be explained.

As they waited for the meal to arrive, Fitzi was given priority on the bathroom. She took a hot shower and shampooed her hair. The steam, the sound of running water, all soothed her. Her neck, still hurting from the quick turns, began to ease up, and her fatigue melted into a delicious languor.

After dinner, Mom and Dad settled on the sofa with a pile of magazines. Clement turned the radio on and napped in an armchair. Rain drummed against the windows.

Clean and cozy in her bathrobe, Fitzi yawned. A quiet evening without lessons stretched ahead. Maybe she would watch TV, or reread an old Rendell book. Maybe she would call Pip or Karen and talk on the phone for a while. She thought of putting out crackers for the pigeons, which she seldom took time to do. But tonight the rain would wash the crackers away.

She decided on a Rendell book, and went into her room to choose one. Almost at once, the phone rang.

Dad answered it. "Hello . . . Oh, gosh . . . I see. No word at all?"

Fitzi realized it was Tiffany's mother. She stood in her doorway to listen.

"Exactly when did you see her last?" Dad was asking.

"When?" Mom interjected.

Dad replied in an undertone, "This morning, at breakfast . . . I'm just filling Donna in, Mrs. Resnick. We're concerned too, believe me, but it just seems as if she's bound to turn up."

"Ask if there's any way we can help," Mom suggested.

Dad did, then held the receiver toward Fitzi. "She wants to talk to you."

Fitzi took the phone.

"Hi, Fitzi." Mrs. Resnick sounded as if she were barely in control, but was trying not to be a pest. "I called the police about Tiffany, but they won't do anything until a person is missing for twenty-four hours. They say she's probably just run off for some reason."

Tiffany? Run off? On a rehearsal day? "Oh," Fitzi responded lamely.

"So I'm still wondering if she said or did anything unusual yesterday."

Fitzi groped through her memory. "Not that I noticed."

"Okay. Well, how did yesterday's rehearsal go? For her, I mean."

"She wasn't doing the quick turns in the first scene as fast as she wanted. They're hard, they snap your neck."

"Was she in pain?"

"Pain? No."

"She seemed—well, carefree?"

"I wouldn't put it like that. We've all got a lot on our minds. The whole cast."

"Sure. Of course you do. Well, maybe something personal was bothering her?"

Fitzi tried to find relevant conversations in the mass of worries, complaints, jokes, and gossip she and Tiffany exchanged day after day, during break, at lunch, passing each other by the stage door. Rehearsals were so hectic that nothing stuck, whole and clean, in her mind.

"I don't think so."

"That crazy fan, did he scare her again?"

Fitzi had gotten so used to the man—to the whole crowd of fans—that she hadn't paid much attention to him lately. "Not that I know of."

Then Mrs. Resnick surprised her by asking, "What about Tiffany's father? Has she mentioned him?"

Fitzi remembered that earlier this week—yesterday? the day before?—Tiffany had seemed gloomy during a rehearsal break. Fitzi had asked her what was wrong.

Tiffany had said, "My dad called me from San Diego. He's starting his vacation. You know we planned to go to Mexico together, just the two of us."

"Yes."

"He made me feel terrible. He said he'd miss me. He'll be eating tortillas and stuff."

"I thought you hated tortillas," Fitzi had said.

"That's not the point. We would have been *together*. He's my *father*."

"Well, sure he is."

"And it would have been so much fun. I just wish I saw him more often."

"If you explain to your mom how you feel, maybe she'd *invite* him to the opening. Then it could be okay."

Tiffany had answered impatiently, "You don't understand. They hate each other."

"Yes, but—"

"I didn't even tell Mom he called. It always puts her in a bad mood."

Now, as Fitzi hesitated, Mrs. Resnick prompted, "Please try to remember." Her voice was taut. "It could be terribly important."

"I *am* trying." Fitzi felt guilty and defensive. She sagged against the wall. "I'm trying," she repeated wretchedly, not sure whether she should tell the truth or not.

Dad took the phone again. Fitzi retreated to her room and closed her door.

She took *The Rendells at Sea* from her bookshelf and lay on her bed to read. It was an exciting story, involving the wreck of a cruise ship. The wealthy Rendells, always poised and gracious, retained their manners even in the lifeboat, though Aurora fussed about the effect of seawater on her diamonds.

The Rendells bobbed on the waves. They sighted an island.

Fitzi read that paragraph again, the waves, the island.

She couldn't concentrate on the book and put it aside, caught in a confusion of other mental pictures: of Tiffany frowning, furious, laughing, scornful, elated.

Was there some hidden meaning in any of these images, some explanation of where Tiffany was?

Should she have told Mrs. Resnick about the phone call from San Diego?

.

When Fitzi and her family arrived at the theater for rehearsal the next morning, two police cars were outside, near the stage door. "Oh, dear," Mom whispered.

They hurried into the theater. Onstage, the cast and crew were gathered in small groups, mystified and troubled.

Mrs. Resnick, her eyes swollen from crying, was talking with Ted and Mr. Ettl.

Fitzi's grandfather stepped forward quickly and asked Mark, "What's happened?"

"There's nothing new, but Tiffany's still missing. A couple of detectives are here, from the Missing Persons Bureau."

A chill of fear went through Fitzi's stomach.

Looking harried, Mr. Ettl asked for the cast's attention. He announced that the police were investigating Tiffany's disappearance and wanted to question some cast members back at headquarters.

"I've given them the names of folks who are especially close to Tiffany." He read off five or six names; Fitzi and Mark headed the list.

.

Fitzi and her parents left the police department around lunchtime. Jerry and Mark were still being questioned. After a quick meal, the Wolpers returned to the theater, to find a dispirited rehearsal going on. With both Gabys absent, the chorus was running listlessly through a dance number.

Fitzi took off her jacket and moved into her place on the stage. She felt wrung out and ready to cry. The detective's questioning had been so thorough that she had revealed every confidence Tiffany had ever entrusted to her. There was no choice; she just hoped some detail might help.

Mr. Ettl seemed unusually considerate of Fitzi. He

started the number over so she could begin at the beginning. Other cast members shifted aside, deferring to her.

Fitzi had a sudden grim realization of her new importance to them. She wasn't just the standby anymore. She was the *only* Gaby, and the opening was only weeks away.

In the middle of the afternoon, Dennis Heath, the show's composer, entered the theater and sat quietly in the third row. Fitzi's tension increased. What was he doing here? Since the first couple of weeks, he hadn't attended rehearsals. It had been reported in *Variety* that with the *Crowd Scene* music finished, he had signed to work on another show.

Fitzi stole looks at him all afternoon. Every time she sang one of Gaby's songs, her chest grew tight.

■

The next day, Tiffany was still missing, and Mr. Heath was out front again. Now Fitzi noticed that he seemed to be paying particular attention to her grandfather, in his role of Bistro Beau.

Like many of the other cast members onstage during the street scenes, Clement sang all the songs along with the chorus, with an occasional line alone. He had a brief duet with Lance. He also had one solo, a semihumorous ballad called "It's Different in the City," which he sang to the country kids.

Clement had a fine tenor voice, especially in the upper register. The last few lines of the song soared. On those notes, his voice was so pure and sweet that the cast remained quiet for a moment or two after he finished, letting the lovely tone die away slowly.

Today, Mr. Ettl sat beside the composer while Clement was singing. They conferred in whispers during the rest of the scene. Always a trouper, Clement went through his song and dialogue and dance numbers exactly as usual, urbane and apparently unflappable.

But during the afternoon break, he and Fitzi and her parents huddled, trying to figure out what was going on.

"The show's probably running long," Clement guessed in an agitated undertone. "It takes forever for that blasted balloon to come down, and the revolving sets don't help any. They may be thinking about cutting my solo."

"No, no," Dad and Fitzi whispered frenzied protests.

"That can't be it." Mom bit her lip. She laid her hand on her father's arm. "Clement, your song's wonderful."

"Bistro Beau is one of the highlights of the show," Dad assured him. "If they cut a word of your part—or a single *note*—it would be madness."

Still, they worried.

·

Mr. Ettl ended the rehearsal early. Neither he nor Mr. Heath said anything at all to Clement.

As the cast tried to leave the theater, they realized the news of Tiffany's disappearance had spread. George, the new security guard at the stage door, was keeping back an avid group of reporters.

"We'll just have to push through them," Dad murmured, hurrying into the crowd. Mom and Fitzi's grand-father followed him, with Fitzi last.

"That's Tiffany's understudy!" a reporter exclaimed.

This brought a hailstorm of questions at Fitzi. Flashbulbs went off in her face. The assault scared her. She covered her face with her hands.

Dad turned and scooped her up in his arms. Clement flagged a cab. The family scrambled into it.

When they reached their apartment building, a TV crew was setting up equipment on the sidewalk, to cover the entrance. Fitzi and her parents scurried inside, leaving Clement to deal with the TV people.

As Dad unlocked the door of their apartment, the phone was ringing. They ignored it, but it didn't stop. Fitzi felt as she sometimes did in bad dreams, as if she were being attacked and couldn't run, couldn't hide.

Mom murmured, "Imagine what Mrs. Resnick must be going through."

The phone kept ringing. Dad said, "Next they'll be pounding on the door."

"How about if we run downstairs to the Logans'?" Mom suggested.

Dad nodded. Like fugitives, the three raced down the stairs and pounded on the Logans' door.

THIRTEEN

To the Wolpers' relief, Pip opened the door immediately. They didn't even have to explain; Pip's mom had gotten the afternoon paper, which contained a police report about Tiffany's disappearance. They had been expecting some kind of commotion in the building.

"Karen's here, too," Pip told Fitzi. "She came over as soon as she heard about it.'

"Donna, Steve, have a seat. Take it easy. I'll get us a drink," Mrs. Logan urged Mom and Dad.

The girls joined Karen in Pip's room. Thin November sunlight lit up the stuffed animals on the twin beds. The lemon glow spilled onto Karen, who was sitting on the floor. Her red hair gleamed around her chubby face.

Fitzi and Pip sat beside her on the flower-patterned rug. Nobody spoke for a minute. Then Pip said, "Tiffany's mom must be a wreck."

Fitzi nodded.

"It said in the paper that nobody had been able to reach her father yet," Karen added.

"Oh? I didn't know that," Fitzi replied.

"Apparently he's on vacation in Mexico, and nobody knows just where."

"Tiffany would have gone with him, except she got the part in *Crowd Scene*." Fitzi added miserably, "I just wish she *had* gone."

There was a long pause. Then, "Maybe she did," Karen suggested.

Fitzi looked up. "What do you mean?"

"Well, she's *missing*," Karen pointed out. "And so is he, in a way."

"Usually, it's the non-custodial parent, in a case like this," Pip said, her snub-nosed face sober. "Remember?" she asked Karen.

Karen nodded.

Fitzi's mind seemed to be lagging. "I don't know what you're talking about."

"We saw a TV show the other night, about missing kids," Pip explained.

"I didn't see it, so spell it out," Fitzi said.

"When the parents are divorced, sometimes one of them

takes the kid without permission," Karen explained. "It amounts to kidnapping, in a legal sense."

"*Kidnapping?* When it's your own father?" Fitzi exclaimed.

"Legally," Pip emphasized. "After all, the kid is *gone,* and nobody knows where."

"Just like Tiffany's gone," Karen added.

"I guess that could happen," Fitzi said slowly. "Except—and this is a *major* except—I just don't believe Tiffany would ditch the show."

Karen leaned on her elbows, her chin in her hands. "Well, the paper mentioned a wild fan, too. A man who stalked Tiffany."

"Yes. Well, he doesn't exactly *stalk* her, but he hangs around the theater. And once Mrs. Resnick saw him near their apartment building. The police asked me when I saw him last, and I'm just not sure."

Pip said, "According to the paper, the police are trying to locate him."

"Seeking him for questioning," Karen corrected.

"The paper said he behaved in a threatening manner," Pip said.

"He did; he's a nut case."

Pip went out to the living room and returned with the newspaper.

"Oh, let me see." Fitzi read the whole account of Tiffany's disappearance, which included the fact that none of the neighbors in the Resnicks' building recalled any disturbance that morning. No one noticed anything unusual.

One woman even thought she saw Tiffany leave for the theater in a limo, as always; however, she wasn't positive. "Might be that's just what I expected to see," she had commented realistically.

"I lean first one way, then the other," Karen said thoughtfully. "The non-custodial parent could be guilty, but the stalker is a real possibility."

Fitzi argued, "There's no way Tiffany would have gone anyplace with that fan, she always ducks away from him. He couldn't have dragged her out of her building without anybody noticing."

"Unless she was—" Pip began hesitantly.

"Unless she was—" Karen echoed, her eyes growing wide.

Fitzi knew what they were thinking. Her skin crawled. "He wouldn't hurt her," she said loudly. "He never acted as if he wanted to hurt her."

There was a somber pause. Then Pip offered reluctantly, "He might have assumed they'd be together in death. If he's deranged and planning suicide. I mean, it's just a thought."

"That's a common idea among stalkers," Karen agreed. "I've read about these creeps."

Pip continued, "He could have wrapped her body in a blanket, and—"

Fitzi put her hands over her ears.

Mrs. Logan called from the other room, "Girls? Would you like some cocoa?"

Fitzi's voice trembled. "Yes, please!"

"Let's change the subject," Karen said.

The sun slid behind the Palisades. The room darkened. Pip turned on her frilly lamps, and played a country music tape. They drank hot cocoa, and talked about a new sci-fi movie.

At dinnertime, Mr. Logan walked Karen home. Just as he returned, Clement came to the Logans' door looking for the Wolpers. He reported that the TV crew out front had given up on catching Fitzi and had disbanded.

"You must stay for dinner with us," Mrs. Logan urged Fitzi and her family.

"We don't want to be a bother," Mom murmured.

"Though, to tell the truth, there's nothing to eat in our place except Shredded Wheat," Dad grinned.

"We can phone U-Call," Clement said, with his endearing smile. "They're often slow, but rather than impose on you, dear lady—"

"Nonsense." Mrs. Logan dismissed this idea. "I'll zap something in the microwave." She bustled off to the kitchen.

"We really don't mind phoning U-Call," Dad offered halfheartedly.

Mr. Logan shook his head. He warned, "You don't want to be opening the door to just anybody."

Dad glanced at Fitzi. "You're right."

The exchange put a new threat in Fitzi's mind: Whatever had happened to Tiffany could happen to her, too.

When she and her family finally went home to their own apartment, they took the rattly old elevator instead of slogging up the stairs. Dad got out first and checked the hall-way, to be sure no reporters were waiting for them.

"All clear," he told the others.

"And so the intrepid quartet entered the military zone," Clement jested.

"Please, Clement, don't try to be funny," Mom objected crossly. "I'm nervous."

"Sorry," he grunted.

As Fitzi was in the bathroom getting ready for bed, she discovered she was bleeding. The sight of the blood, after the fears of the day, sent panic through her. Then she realized she was menstruating.

This was her first period. She would have to get some stuff from Mom. Pads? Tampons?

She thought of the afternoon in acrobatics class, months and months ago, when she and Tiffany had talked about menstruation. She remembered Tiffany's face, streaked with sweat; and a terrible wave of loss swept over her.

A tumble of other memories assailed her: of Tiffany zipping down Riverside Drive on a skateboard, a pow-erhouse on wheels . . . Tiffany in a brown wig, trying out for Mark's soap opera . . . Tiffany when she was younger, popping energetically out of a foil wrapper as a corn kernel in a popcorn commercial.

And in this avalanche of memory and loss, she had a sudden icy certainty that Tiffany was dead. She began to sob.

"Fitz!" Mom called through the bathroom door in alarm. "What's the matter?"

Fitzi put on her bathrobe and opened the door, still sobbing. She saw her father and grandfather standing behind Mom, everybody upset. "She's dead." She pushed past them to her own room and flung herself on the bed.

Mom followed. "Fitz, Fitz—"

"I know you don't believe me, but she's dead."

Mom sat on the side of the bed and hugged her hard. "Honey, you don't know that."

"I do! I do!"

"How?"

"I just feel it. I'm positive. She's gone, and she's never coming back." Her cries rose in a high wail.

"Okay. Okay," Mom soothed and patted her.

Fitzi blurted, "I've got my period, too."

"Oh." Mom left the room and returned with a box of pads. She closed the door behind her and handed the box to Fitzi matter-of-factly.

Fitzi went into the bathroom. A minute later, with the pad securely fastened, she began to feel more in control. Her mother's no-fuss response steadied her.

They sat side by side on the bed. Fitzi asked the question that had bugged her for years: "What do you wear under your leotard? At these times?"

"I wear tampons, and latex-lined pants, if I have to. And change them a lot."

"Did you ever have an accident?"

"Not when I was performing. Just once or twice when I was sitting around, not thinking about it."

"Were you embarrassed?"

Mom answered slowly, "Well, it's a private thing. Nobody wants it to be public. But no, I wasn't really embarrassed."

"I wish tomorrow was Sunday. I don't know what to wear to rehearsal."

"Oh, that's no problem. Wear whatever you're comfortable in. Soon you may want a bra, but there's no rush."

They sat together quietly. After a few minutes, Fitzi wiped the last tears off her damp face. She smiled. "Thanks, Mom."

FOURTEEN

On their way to the theater next morning, the limo driver asked, "Anything new about Tiffany Resnick?"

"No," Dad replied. "I just called her mother and there are no leads yet."

"So what's your theory?" the driver asked chattily. "Think she was kidnapped, or she split?"

Fitzi's grandfather answered with some irritation, "We truly have no theories of any kind."

As they approached the theater, Fitzi saw a group of TV and newspaper people at the stage door, along with a crowd of curious onlookers. A flash of dread went through her. She begged, "Can't we go in some other way?"

Dad took her two hands firmly in his strong ones. His thin face was intense under the black hair that fringed his forehead. "Courage," he said simply.

"Why?" Fitzi demanded wildly. "Don't we have enough to worry about without dealing with *them?*"

Clement remarked, "You can't keep running, my girl. The press and the public own a piece of us, like it or not."

Horns blew. "I'll just drive around the block while you folks decide," the driver said.

"Do that," Dad told him.

Mom said gently, "Fitz, you're news now. The whole show is. The whole cast. But especially you. It's a story, the young understudy who may become a star—"

"If Tiffany's *dead,* you mean?" Hysterical tears ran down Fitzi's cheeks. "It's *ghoulish!* I bet they *hope* she's dead! Then they can ask us how we feel about it."

"Listen, I'm sorry if I acted nosy before," the driver apologized with a sheepish look in the mirror.

"No, no," Mom assured him distractedly.

They pulled up to the stage door a second time. The limo stopped. People turned. Fitzi realized she had to go through with it; get out of the car, answer questions. Mom gave her a Kleenex.

Fitzi mopped off her face and told her family miserably, "I can't think of anything but obvious stuff."

"That's what they expect," her grandfather bucked her

up. "That's all they want. Just say you're praying for Tiffany's safe return, and they'll be satisfied."

Fitzi stumbled out of the car, into the crowd. Questions flew at her like arrows. She answered every one exactly the way Clement had suggested. Eventually she made it inside.

She saw Mark, already onstage, and walked toward him. Briefly, he took her hand. "Hello."

"Hello." She smiled bleakly.

"Okay, good. Glad you're here, Fitzi," Mr. Ettl said. "Places for first and second scenes, please."

Trailed by Bernie, Mark moved to the country scene, while Fitzi and the others got ready for their Champs-Élysées number. Fitzi was wearing a warm-up suit and her first tampon. She was aware of the change in her body; a woman's body now, not a child's.

The rehearsal went better than it had yesterday or the day before. She and Mark blended their moves and their personalities more smoothly. "Great chemistry there," Mr. Ettl praised them. "Doing great."

But there were bad trouble spots for Fitzi, and she was beginning to realize she might actually have to play this part. Soon they would start rehearsing with the full orchestra. There would be costume fittings, lighting rehearsals, increased pressure every hour, until that opening night curtain went up. And even beyond.

If Tiffany wasn't found, Fitzi would be carrying eight shows a week in a major role. The responsibility seemed crushing.

Later in the morning, the composer, Dennis Heath, arrived. Again he watched attentively from the third row of the theater.

Clement performed as flawlessly as ever, but Fitzi started making dumb mistakes. Lyrics of a song, which she had known perfectly before, escaped her completely. Her feet seemed to tangle in a series of dance steps; she should have been standing still when Mark said his next lines. Instead, she was tap-dancing busily all over the stage.

Mark exploded in an annoyed whisper, "Pull yourself together, will you? You upstaged me."

"I didn't mean to!"

She stumbled on.

The cast had already rehearsed the scene where the country kids questioned Bistro Beau about Paris, and he had answered them with his solo, "It's Different in the City." But then the composer asked Mr. Ettl, "Could we take Clement Dale's number again?"

"Sure. Clement?" Mr. Ettl called Fitzi's grandfather back to center stage.

The rehearsal pianist started up the music again. Clement repeated it. After the last lovely, haunting notes, Mr. Heath smiled and nodded. "Thank you."

He and the director called Ted over. The three men conferred as the cast waited. Fitzi glanced at her grandfather. He had exited to the wings, swinging his cane debonairly. Now he stood alone, dabbing at the sweat on his upper lip with a Kleenex.

Mr. Ettl said, "Okay. Lunchtime, folks."

Ted sent out for sandwiches and drinks for the whole cast, so they wouldn't have to cope with reporters. To Fitzi, whose childhood had been spent largely as a street performer, it was stifling to spend so many hours indoors. Even in school she had been able to go out for recess and lunch. She sat with her mother, glumly eating her sandwich.

By the afternoon rehearsal break, she longed for fresh air. As soon as Mr. Ettl gave them fifteen minutes off, she headed for the door to the back alley. Still stung by Mark's criticism, she hoped he would follow her and make peace. But he was sitting with Clement and Lance, absorbed in their endless flow of lively stories.

She cracked open the alley door and peered out cautiously, wary of reporters. Except for the usual huddled figure in one of the doorways, nobody was there.

The cool November air felt good. She walked through the alley out to the street, to the bustling midafternoon stir of the city. On the sidewalk, everybody was hurrying someplace, paying no attention to her. Fitzi enjoyed the sensation of just being alone, unnoticed.

After a few minutes, she turned back into the alley. Before she could reach the theater door, someone rushed from another doorway, startling her. Confused and scared, she realized it must be the person she had often seen huddled in the alley and had never recognized.

Now she saw him clearly. He loomed over her, cutting

her off from the door into the theater. It was the burly man who waited so often for Tiffany, her most persistent fan.

Horrified, Fitzi turned and started to run back through the alley to the street. He caught her in a few swift strides. One of his arms gripped her around the wrist. She got out the beginning of a scream, but almost immediately, his big hand clapped across her mouth and she couldn't utter a sound.

"No, no," he was muttering urgently. "No no no." He pulled her farther away from the street. Scrambling to keep her footing, shaking with panic, she tried to figure out where she was from the theater door. It was probably only a couple of yards, but in his powerful grip, it might as well have been miles.

He maneuvered her so that her back was pinned against the brick wall of the theater. Facing him, she smelled his unwashed body. What was happening? Was he going to kill her? Drag her off someplace? Kidnap her? First Tiffany, now her?

Fitzi struggled, trying to kick him, but he was too close for her to get much leverage. She gave him a smothered yelp, but then he clamped her mouth tighter.

"Listen," he implored. "You listen."

Rough though he was, his tone took the edge off her panic. She fought for enough calm to get oriented, to sort out what he was doing. He didn't seem to be dragging her anyplace, or holding her harder than necessary to keep her from running away.

"I have to tell you something," he went on, still in that imploring tone.

Fitzi stared into his wild face. There was a craziness in it, but not the menace she had seen when he was trying to protect Tiffany.

"Listen," he entreated again.

Swallowing, breathing hard, Fitzi nodded.

"You will?" He seemed to be asking for a promise.

She nodded again.

Slowly he removed his hand from over her mouth, ready to stifle any cry for help. Fitzi made no sound. He put one hand on each of her shoulders, holding her against the wall, but not hurting her.

"I saw them take her," he said hoarsely. To Fitzi's astonishment, his eyes, under bushy dark brows, filled with tears.

"You did?" Fitzi whispered.

"I didn't see the one who was driving, but the other— I knew the other."

"Who was it?"

"Him who used to be at the stage door."

"The security guard?"

He affirmed eagerly, "Right, him. The young one."

Fitzi remembered the tussle at the stage door when he had tried to get in. "You mean Duke?" she asked, unsure whether this talk was making sense. "Duke took Tiffany?"

"Yes! Yes! Him and somebody else, in a car."

Fitzi prayed to say the right thing, to ask the right questions. "From where?"

"Outside her apartment building, that morning. The day she disappeared. I always watch her leave for rehearsal." He added with lunatic pride, "I watch out for her."

"Yes," Fitzi whispered. "You were watching that morning, and the car came? Like always?"

He shook his head. "It came earlier. And not the same car. A shorter car."

"Not a limo."

"No. Gray, with dark windows, but a different kind of car, I don't know—" He looked helpless and agitated.

"That's okay," Fitzi said. "And you saw Duke?"

"Yes, he got out of the front. Not the driver's side, the other. He spoke to Tiffany. Seemed as if he had to talk her into getting in."

"Maybe because it wasn't the car she was used to?"

"Yes, yes. Wrong car. Then he got out and spoke to her. She got in, and he jumped in the back beside her. Somebody else was in the front and drove them away."

"Who was the driver?"

"Darkened windows! Darkened windows!" The man's agitation increased; he was desperate to be understood. "Darkened—"

"So you couldn't see the driver, but you're sure about Duke?"

He nodded emphatically. "I know him. I saw his face. It was him. Ran across the street, wanted to stop them—"

"Who ran? You did?"

Again the burly man's eyes glistened with tears. "But they drove away too fast, I couldn't catch them. Then—

then—" He raved incoherently. Fitzi couldn't make out what he was trying to tell her.

She stopped him, pleading, "Wait. Please. Talk slower. They drove away, and—what?"

He gripped her shoulders harder for extra emphasis. She winced. "The car went the wrong way." He was almost shouting. "Not downtown, like other mornings. It went around the corner. Wrong car, wrong way."

Fitzi felt numb, unable to interpret any of this. "You should tell the police."

"No, *you* tell them."

"But—"

"No." The off-kilter glaze of craziness was on his face again. "I stay away from police. They don't like me."

"But—"

"*You* tell them." He shook her roughly.

Fitzi got frightened again. "I will! Let go of me!"

He pushed her against the wall. She staggered, almost fell. He ran from the alley to the street and vanished.

F I F T E E N

Fitzi stumbled into the theater, where the cast was still on break.

Mom was practicing her juggling, with the blue and green balls she would use in the show. Dad was showing young Bernie a mime butterfly chase. Lance was telling a story about Yakima Canutt, the awesome movie stunt man who staged the chariot race in *Ben Hur*.

Fogged by shock and bewilderment, Fitzi had a sense of nightmare; of swinging from one dream state to another. The make-believe in the theater and the grotesque scene in the alley seemed equally unreal.

Her grandfather followed up Lance's anecdote with a

tale about Canutt's sons, who had staged horse battles for *Camelot*. Mark caught sight of Fitzi. He got up quickly and strode to where she stood. "Fitzi, what's wrong? You're white as a ghost."

She stammered, "A m-man in the alley—"

After she had told him everything, he took her hand and led her to Mr. Ettl. Mom and Dad and Clement converged on them.

When he had heard the story, Mr. Ettl ordered George to lock the door to the alley, and to secure the rest of the theater. Dad called the police; they arrived within minutes. They searched the theater, the alley, and the surrounding area for the man, but couldn't find him.

A detective came to question Fitzi.

Ted and Mr. Ettl, distraught at the continued interruptions to rehearsals, decided to run through part of Act Three, a succession of specialty numbers. Even as she answered what the detective was asking, Fitzi heard the music, *her* music for the solo dance. With a bitter pang, she saw Alix Ashton taking her place.

·

That evening, Dad called Fitzi's tutor and suspended her lessons until after the show opened.

"Why don't you see if Pip can come up for a while?" Mom suggested.

"What for?" Fitzi asked dully. She had showered, eaten, and was half-asleep in her bathrobe.

"For Pete's sake! To relax and talk to an old friend," Mom told her briskly. "Just for an hour."

"She'll ask if there's anything new, and I'll have to tell her about today."

"Maybe it would be good to talk it over with her," Mom said gently.

"Why?"

Mom put her arm around her. "Just to touch base with the real world."

Fitzi said, "When I got in from the alley, I felt as if nothing was real."

"I guess we all wish it wasn't."

"Do you think what that man told me was true?"

"I have no idea, Fitz."

"He could have just been covering for himself, if he's the guilty one."

"He could have."

Fitzi bit her thumb. "Why did he tell *me* about it? I mean, why me?"

"Probably because you were the one who came out into the alley alone. I imagine he's really scared of most people."

"What if I hadn't gone out there? What if nobody had?"

"Well, you did. And you told the police. That's all you can do, hon. Now we just have to wait."

Clement snapped on the TV. "Anyone mind if I watch the news? Fitzi?"

She sighed. "No, go ahead."

After news from the Middle East and a verdict in a racial murder trial, there was an update about Tiffany. Apparently Mr. Resnick had learned of his daughter's disappearance by reading a New York newspaper in Mexico. He was flying to New York.

The announcer also reported that the police were rumored to be seeking Duke Kranz, former security guard at the theater, for questioning. A headshot of Duke was flashed on the screen. No other details were given.

Fitzi didn't call Pip. She felt as if she couldn't stand one more question about Tiffany, one more comment, one more theory. She lay awake in bed for a long time, thinking of good times before she had ever heard of *Crowd Scene*.

One day last spring she and Pip had gone to the Central Park zoo. They had flung off their sweaters and tied them around their waists, glorying in the mildness of the weather. They had bought hot dogs and had eaten them on a bench near the seals.

Fitzi remembered just how it had been: the wonderful smell of mustard and steaming rolls; the clear spring calls of birds; a little kid hollering as he spilled his caramel corn.

·

Somehow Fitzi and her family got up next morning, dressed, dragged themselves to rehearsal. It was raining.

Somehow they got through most of the day.

Then, in the middle of the afternoon, Mr. Heath appeared again. He and Mr. Ettl drew Clement aside, while Ted kept the rehearsal going.

Fitzi and her mom exchanged scared glances. They both realized what this conversation could mean. The composer and director might be cutting Clement's solo from the show.

No, Fitzi cried silently. *Please.*

This part meant so much to Clement—his first Broadway role since his stroke, and maybe his best part ever.

Fitzi and Mom passed each other, dancing around the chorus line. "They can't *do* that!" Mom protested in a furious whisper. "He's so *good!*"

Fitzi nodded emphatically.

But they both knew even good things got cut, when a show ran too long. In *Crowd Scene,* the orchestral arrangements would take more time than the rehearsal pianist's music. Sets, lighting, costume changes: all were complicated; and later, with an audience out front, laughter and applause would lengthen the play further.

Fitzi began to have a sick certainty that "It's Different in the City" was out. Whenever she could, she glanced at Clement's face, dreading the dismay she expected to see.

But as the director and composer talked to him, Fitzi's grandfather smiled. His skin flushed with pleasure. The long, roguish dimple flashed in his cheek. Relief washed over Fitzi; he looked happy; more than happy.

At the next break, she and her parents besieged her grandfather.

"Tell us, quick! What *happened?*"

Clement's handsome face shone with excitement. "He's writing a new song for me! They're *adding* another solo for Bistro Beau in the third act. He said my voice"—the words were suddenly unsteady—"he said my voice was celestial. Pretty high-flown, if you ask me, but—"

"Well, it *is!* I'm not a bit surprised," Mom lied enthusiastically.

"Anyway, he's got some ideas—a few lyrics—didn't tell me what they were—"

They all exclaimed, asked questions, hugged Clement. Lance had rushed over. They shared the news with him. Mark joined them. "Something good going on here?"

Fitzi and her grandfather interrupted each other, explaining one more time.

"Oh, Clement." Mom hugged her father, glowing. "This started off being such an awful day, and now look!"

Dad put in, "This is why we should never be discouraged. That lucky rainbow may be just around the corner!"

The rehearsal continued. Fitzi and her family were infused with fresh energy. They abandoned themselves to excitement, and their performances had never been better.

Around four o'clock, Mr. Ettl was summoned to the phone. When he returned, he stopped everything, and asked for everybody's attention. His demeanor was grave.

A scared hush fell on the theater.

"Tiffany's been found," Mr. Ettl announced, his heavy shoulders bowed, head thrust forward. His tone was so sorrowful that Fitzi went icy with fear.

"Is she dead?" someone asked quietly.

"She's alive, but she's hurt. They've taken her to the hospital." Mr. Ettl spread his hands in resignation. "That's all I know."

S I X T E E N

Fitzi stood in the hospital hall outside Tiffany's room, waiting her turn to go in. She held a bunch of daisies and pink carnations that she and Mom had bought from a street seller.

"Honey, don't you want to sit down?" Mom asked her softly.

Fitzi shook her head. She was too jumpy to sit. Mom settled into a chair in the waiting area.

Since she was found two days ago, Tiffany hadn't been strong enough to have any visitors except her parents, and

Fitzi dreaded seeing her. She knew Tiffany had been beaten by her two kidnappers. They had wanted her to record a tape, urging her family to provide ransom money. The cassette, and a note specifying a dropoff point for the money, were to be sent to Mrs. Resnick.

But Tiffany had proved unexpectedly feisty. As soon as she had realized she was being kidnapped, she had kicked and struggled and refused to do what she was told, including making the tape.

At first Duke and his accomplice had simply bound and gagged her, waiting for her to break down. When she didn't, they had tried force.

"That wild man in the alley told you the truth," Mom had said to Fitzi.

Duke had used the information he had as security guard to figure out Tiffany's schedule and get her address and phone number. His accomplice, who had a police record for stealing cars, had ripped off a gray Mercury Grand Marquis from a parking lot in Westchester County. While the car was smaller than the Lincoln Town Car that usually picked Tiffany up, it resembled it.

The morning of her disappearance, Duke phoned Tiffany just after her mother left for work. He said he had his old job back, and that Mr. Ettl had asked him to call because he wanted some cast members to start rehearsal half an hour earlier that day. He said he would also call the limo company and have Tiffany picked up earlier.

"Instead, of course, he and his pal picked her up in the stolen Mercury," Mom had explained.

"Didn't she think it was weird when Duke showed up with the car?" Fitzi asked.

"I guess she did, but he talked her into it somehow. They drove her to upper Westchester, to a rented cabin, and ditched the car about half a mile away. The police found it there. And they had an anonymous tip from somebody who saw Duke's picture on TV. They traced him to the cabin."

"After more than four whole days," Fitzi groaned.

"Honey, she's alive, and she's going to get better," Mom reminded her emphatically.

Now, waiting to see Tiffany, Fitzi squeezed the bunch of flowers and bit her lip anxiously.

Tiffany's door opened. Mr. and Mrs. Resnick came out. They looked strained and sad, but at least they weren't fighting.

"Hello, Fitzi," Mrs. Resnick murmured. "She's looking forward to seeing you. Don't stay too long."

"I won't."

Mom said, "Go ahead in, hon."

"Aren't you coming too?"

"No. You two can talk easier alone. Just give her my love."

"Okay."

Fitzi prepared an expression, as if she were auditioning for the part of cheerful visitor. She held the flowers in front of her like a shield, and went into the room.

For an instant she thought there had been a mistake, the girl in the bed looked so different from Tiffany. Her face was thinner, and strangely pale, with dark bruises around one eye. There was a cut on one of her cheeks, a bandage on her chin. And, most pathetic to Fitzi, her hair hung lankly around her shoulders, combed, but uncurled.

Every night of her life, since she was about six years old, Tiffany had put up her hair on fat rollers. Her torrent of curls, pinned casually on her head, seemed as characteristic of her as her hands or feet. The only thing that looked like Tiffany was a lacy blue nylon bedjacket, tied with an extravagant bow in front.

"I know I look terrible, and I don't care," she said sullenly.

"I don't care either." Fitzi's voice trembled. "It's wonderful just to see you."

She moved closer to the bed, not knowing what to do with her bunch of flowers. The room was filled with fancy arrangements and blooming plants.

"I brought you these." She held them forward awkwardly.

"There are some vases by the sink."

She found one, filled it with water, stuck the bouquet in, and set it on the windowsill. Feeling horribly at a loss, she made this take as long as she could. Maybe she had made a mistake in coming. Tiffany didn't seem particularly glad to see her.

She stood beside the bed, mustering a smile.

"You can sit down if you want."

"Okay." Fitzi pulled a chair away from the wall and sat in it. There was a heavy silence. A clock ticked.

Tiffany stirred weakly against the pillows. "My mother said you were rehearsing when I was found."

"Yes, we were."

"Did you talk about me every day I was missing?"

Fitzi was surprised by the question. Under the other girl's pallor and weakness, she saw an avidity, as if she were trying to fill in that empty stolen time.

She answered quickly, "Sure we did. Of course."

"What did you say?"

"Well, mostly we wondered where you were and what had happened."

Tiffany smiled faintly. "You ran through different scenarios?"

"Yeah, every one there is. And then some."

"I was in a tacky old cabin."

"I know."

"They hit me." She touched her bruised face.

"Your mom told us."

Tiffany turned her face away. She began to cry.

Fitzi reached out delicately and laid a hand on her shoulder. The blue nylon bedjacket was slippery, its lace stiff.

"When he was the security guard, Duke was always nice to me," Tiffany said bitterly through her tears.

"I remember."

"He was setting me up."

"I guess so. How did he explain being in the car that morning?"

"He said he had phoned me from his apartment—about coming to rehearsal early—and since he lived just a few blocks away, he had asked the limo service to pick him up too. He said the service had to send a different car and driver because of the time change."

"Well, that would make sense."

Tears slid from the corners of her eyes. "It all seemed a little peculiar. His getting his job back, the change in rehearsal time, the driver picking him up. But Duke wasn't a stranger. We all knew him."

"When did you realize something was wrong?"

"Oh, right away. The car turned west. We went to the West Side Highway instead of downtown toward the theater. I started yelling at them to let me out. They tied me up and gagged me. And there were people right outside the car, going to work, so near—but they couldn't see me through the dark windows." She began to cry convulsively.

"You don't have to talk about it anymore."

"They had to stop to pay a toll, and I tried to make noises—they had me on the floor of the backseat—I thought I might die there. Did you think I was dead?"

"Sometimes."

"It's over, though. I'm here."

"Yes, you are. We still talk about you a lot at rehearsals." Fitzi searched her mind frantically for another topic. "The hot-air balloon works now."

"Oh, yes?" A tiny flicker of interest showed in Tiffany's blurred eyes. "How's Bernie doing with it?"

"Pretty well. He was terrified the first few descents, but now he seems okay."

Tiffany nodded. She looked exhausted.

"I'd better go." Fitzi got up. She had refrained from mentioning the growing suspense about when Tiffany would be well enough to return to work. With the opening only a little more than three weeks away, it was a question everyone wondered about.

Hoping to get a clue, she said, "Everybody's looking forward to seeing you. We missed you every minute."

Tiffany nodded negligently. "Well, I may go to the opening."

Stunned, Fitzi burst out, "The *opening?* What about rehearsals?"

"I'm not returning to the show." She gave Fitzi a pallid smile. "I told my parents, but they don't believe it yet."

Fitzi protested, "Tiffany, I don't believe it either."

"Well, it's true. I don't care about the show anymore. Something happened." She moved restlessly in the bed. "Something changed. Inside me." She laughed grimly. "They knocked a hole in me and my talent flew out."

"Talent doesn't go away like that."

"No? Well, then I don't know how to explain it. But you can tell Mr. Ettl and the others. I'm not coming back."

S E V E N T E E N

Tiffany went home two days later. Her parents notified Mr. Ettl that she would not return to rehearsals or appear in the show. She was out, definitely.

"I wonder if there'll be a contract dispute?" Clement mused.

"I doubt it. Everybody has so much sympathy for Tiffany, after all she's been through. And she has a super understudy," Mom said brightly, giving Fitzi a hug.

During the time Tiffany was missing, Fitzi's family, like everybody else, had been so concerned about Tiffany that there wasn't much room for anything else. Now, though,

Fitzi could see that her parents were allowing themselves to be thrilled over the prospect of her promotion to a leading role.

Suddenly it wasn't Tiffany's big chance anymore. It was Fitzi's big chance.

And Clement's.

He got his new song. Mr. Heath gave it to him at rehearsal, and went over it with him, away from the rest of the cast.

That night, Clement brought it to the family dinner table. He was too excited to eat. Holding the music, he hummed it for Fitzi and her parents. Called "Closing Time," it was a wistful melody in a minor key, ideally suited to his voice.

"Oh, Clement, that's lovely," Mom sighed.

"Good range," Dad commented. "Plenty of high notes."

"What's the title mean?" Fitzi asked.

"It's closing time at the cabaret. They're putting the song in Act Three, right after the big dance number."

Fitzi thought of that number. Bistro Beau and the Bartender were inside the cabaret, with a throng of revelers. Outside, street performers entertained the passing crowds. Neon signs for cafes and nightclubs lit up the night.

Clement went on, "People drift out of the cabaret. Finally only Bistro Beau remains, with the Bartender."

Fitzi pictured her grandfather and Lance alone on the deserted set.

"The signs go off, one by one. The crowds thin out. A few street people are still there—jugglers, magicians, and so on—"

Mom groaned, "Oh, spare me. I mean, it's super, Clement, but does it mean we all have to learn new moves?"

"Yes, yes, of course," Clement brushed this off impatiently. "Naturally the action will change. Can't make an omelette without breaking eggs. Maybe you can work in a few more magic tricks."

Dad murmured to his wife, "When life hands you a lemon, make lemonade."

Mom buried her head in her hands.

"Do you think Gaby'll have to do anything different?" Fitzi asked anxiously. It was only three weeks before the opening, and she had troubles enough.

"I don't know," her grandfather answered absently. He hummed a few more bars of the song.

Dad reassured Fitzi, "Seems to me a kid would be too young to be around a cabaret at closing time."

"Gaby leads a rough life," Fitzi reminded him, her voice trembling.

But it developed that all the younger players would exit before Clement's solo. Inside the cabaret, the Bartender would wipe down the bar. Bistro Beau would lift his glass in a final toast, and amble out into the street. The crowds and street performers would go. Finally Bistro Beau would stroll away from the cabaret. The Bartender would lock the door behind him and exit.

The only other person left onstage would be Dad, the juggler.

Bistro Beau would move down to center stage, a spotlight on him, darkness on the rest of the set. Behind him, the juggler would stand on top of a flight of steps. In a white leotard and with white face makeup, he would appear almost to float in the night.

Slowly, Dad would juggle luminous white balls, while Clement sang: "Another evening gone, the laughter dying . . . the toasts are drunk, we've said our last good-bye . . ." Each verse expressed regret at happiness passing, and ended with the words, "It's closing time."

The haunting song showcased Clement's talents perfectly. The staging, with the strange white juggler glimmering in the darkness, gave it a mysterious quality.

Burt Janus quickly complained that adding the song in Act Three, so near the end of the show, would detract from his own performance in the previous cabaret scene.

Ormelle suggested that *she* be the one to stay on alone in the cabaret, and sing "Closing Time."

The chorus muttered about learning new moves. Several cast members wondered if the show was now too long, and worried that their scenes would later be cut.

"This old guy is almost washed up, and they've given him one of the best numbers in the show," somebody grumbled.

With a flare of rage, Fitzi knew that her grandfather overheard this. She was hurt and embarrassed for him.

But his eyes glinted like blue steel in their net of wrinkles. Ignoring the comment, he strode away. He continued to polish every note, every nuance.

.

Rehearsals ground on. Fitzi worked endlessly on Gaby's tricky fast turns in Act One, getting them perfect. Then she began to have trouble with a song in Act Two. It was only two weeks before the opening; then only a week and a half.

She had costume fittings for the role of Gaby. As Tiffany's standby, she would have been fitted for this costume in any case, but now, as the merry, ragged dress was pinned in place, she had a heavy sense of how different everything had become.

"And you told us you'd never have to play that part," Pip teased her one evening as she spent a rare hour at the Logans'.

Alix Ashton, fitted for the dance number in Act Three, smirked during rehearsals, and actually began giving autographs outside the stage door.

"Suddenly she's acting like a star," Fitzi told Mark furiously.

.

Once Tiffany was found, media interest in *Crowd Scene* waned. The PR man maintained some suspense by refusing to make any announcement about whether or not she would be in the show, but reporters no longer thronged around the theater.

Fans still gathered in the late afternoon, though. Fitzi watched for the man whose information had led to Tiffany's rescue, and had put Duke and his accomplice in jail. But she never saw him again.

.

Each day after rehearsal, Fitzi and her parents stopped in at the Resnicks' for a few minutes, to see Tiffany. The grown-ups usually talked quietly with Mr. and Mrs. Resnick in the living room. Fitzi was taken into the bedroom where Tiffany, in a nylon robe, stretched on a chaise like a movie queen.

The visits seemed peculiar to Fitzi. Tiffany looked much better than she had in the hospital. Her face was rounding out again. The bruise around her eye had faded; the cut on her cheek was healing. The bandage was gone from her chin. Her hair, freshly bleached, curled luxuriantly again, and was pinned on top of her head, a few provocative tendrils dangling.

But she was being treated like a chronic invalid, or maybe like a spoiled infant. While Fitzi sat humbly on an ottoman beside the chaise, Tiffany kept asking her to fetch things; a comb, a glass of water, a dainty afghan.

"Are you paralyzed?" Fitzi asked in exasperation, rebelling. "Get your own afghan." It was a week before the scheduled opening of the show. She felt nervous and cross, exhausted from the long day of rehearsals, and in no mood to coddle somebody who looked fairly healthy.

"Well! If it's too much trouble, never mind," Tiffany retorted sulkily. She called her mother, who gladly brought the afghan. Then Mr. Resnick offered to go out for ice cream.

"Well, you've certainly got them where you want them," Fitzi commented when Mr. and Mrs. Resnick had left the room.

"It's about time, isn't it?" Tiffany demanded. "When has my dad ever been around before, doing what I want?"

Taken aback, Fitzi mumbled, "Not for a while."

"Never! Even before he and Mom were divorced, they got their kicks out of fighting with each other—over me, over money, over anything. This is the most peaceful we've ever been."

"How long is he staying in New York?"

"For *weeks*. It's marvelous. He's got a lot of his vacation days still. Then he's planning on some job leave. And all for me." Dropping the languid pretense, Tiffany sat up straight on the chaise. She laughed her big, full-throated laugh. "It's not going to kill him to buy ice cream and be Mr. Nice Guy for a change!"

The laugh was miraculous; suddenly the old Tiffany broke through the veil of sickly glamour. She looked confident, vigorous, full of chutzpah.

Fitzi couldn't help laughing with her. "But you're ordering your mom around, too."

"No kidding!" Tiffany exclaimed with a wicked grin. She added seriously, "My mother never took enough time off from her job to do much for me. Maybe she owes me."

Fitzi thought about it. "How do your parents feel about you quitting the show?"

"These days, I can do no wrong," Tiffany reported with satisfaction. "They both said they'd support whatever decision I made, and they have."

"But how long can you lie around and eat ice cream? Aren't you *bored?*"

"Nope." Slightly apologetically, Tiffany added, "I do exercises in the morning."

"Wow, how can you stand the pace?"

Tiffany fiddled with a bow on her robe. "I know it can't last forever, but I need it right now."

Fitzi joked, "Think about how great life was before! Your folks fought, you and I fought, everything was normal."

Tiffany chuckled. "Back then, you told me we were all weird."

"Oh, weird, sure. But *normally* weird."

▪

That evening Fitzi's parents went out to dinner and to the opening of a friend's show.

Fitzi and her grandfather ate together. Then he played some golden oldies on his record player. Together they sat and listened to Vic Damone, Frank Sinatra, Nat King Cole. Clement hummed along, waving a hand slightly, in time to the music. Fitzi stared into space.

After a while, her grandfather reached in his pocket. He held a penny toward her in his hand. "Penny."

"What?" Roused from her reverie, Fitzi looked blankly at the penny. "What's that for?"

"Your thoughts."

"Oh. Well, I was thinking of what Mr. Ettl said on the first day of rehearsals. About hard choices."

"Ah, yes."

"I guess we have to make a lot of those, don't we? Everybody."

He studied her face keenly. "Yes. We do."

The next night, during her visit to Tiffany, Fitzi asked her, "Remember when we heard each other on lines?"

"Sure."

"You said my interpretation was wrong."

Tiffany shrugged. "Maybe not wrong. Just wimpy."

"I wish you'd come to rehearsal tomorrow and see how I'm doing."

Tiffany dismissed the idea flatly. "That's Mr. Ettl's problem."

Keeping down her rising temper, Fitzi said, "Actually it's *my* problem, and I hoped you'd help. I've helped you plenty of times."

"I never needed advice!"

"No, no." Fitzi swallowed her anger. "Not advice. But we did go over those Gaby lines very, very often."

"And I'll bet you're glad now," Tiffany retorted.

"Absolutely. You were right," Fitzi agreed hastily. "But your input would mean a lot to me."

"I don't want to go to rehearsal. I don't ever want to see that theater again." She leaned back dramatically and shut her eyes. "I've been through more than you'll ever know. I don't want to be reminded of what it took out of me."

Looking at Tiffany, Fitzi almost believed her, and felt a wave of sorrow. It was true that Fitzi could not imagine being captured, beaten, terrorized by the thought she might never get home again. And with all that, Tiffany claimed her talent was gone.

But it wasn't. Tiffany still seemed to be playing a part, ably and effectively. It was just the *wrong* part.

Fitzi steeled herself. "How long are we supposed to pity you?" she asked cruelly. She picked up her jacket and left.

EIGHTEEN

Fitzi and her family arrived at rehearsal promptly next morning as usual. Mark came in a minute later, then Bernie and his mother, then Alix Ashton. A few stragglers still hadn't appeared. Fitzi watched the stage door anxiously. The last few cast members hurried in.

Ted called, "Okay, places for the first scene, please, everybody."

Disappointed, Fitzi took her place. So did her parents, her grandfather, Lance, and all the others. Janus and Ormelle waited in the wings for their entrance cues.

Then three people entered the back of the theater. They walked up the long, long center aisle, approaching slowly.

Fitzi did not recognize them immediately. She had expected Tiffany to come alone, as before, and through the stage door. But when the three were only a few rows away from the stage, Mr. Ettl exclaimed with a big smile, "Look who's here!"

Walking up the aisle with one of her parents on each side of her, Tiffany smiled wanly. Mr. Ettl leaped down from the stage and ran to her; grabbed and hugged her. Ted, and several members of the cast and crew, streamed up the aisle to kiss and welcome her.

"I told Fitzi I'd come and watch for a while," Tiffany explained in a frail voice. "If no one minds."

"*Mind?* We're delighted," Mr. Ettl assured her. "Wonderful, wonderful!"

When the rehearsal was finally about to get underway, Mr. and Mrs. Resnick sat out front. Sagging slightly, looking infinitely fragile, Tiffany climbed the few stairs to the stage, so she could watch from the wings. Ted quickly fetched a chair and offered it to her. With a wispy sigh, Tiffany sank into it, just offstage.

"Places, please, everybody," Ted said again.

The piano player banged out the start of the opening number. Brilliant smiles streaked across every face. Mom began to juggle her blue and green balls, Dad whipped forth his magic props, Clement and Lance strutted toward each other, swinging their sticks debonairly. The chorus sang, "It's a beautiful day on the Champs-Élysées . . ."

and Fitzi made her entrance, tossing her head, kicking high, kicking low.

She joined lustily in the song: "Anything can happen—"

This was the scene she had worked on harder than any other. As she circled the chorus line, her hands coquettishly on her hips, she saw that Tiffany had risen from her chair and was craning forward to watch. Her face was flushed.

There was a lot of dialogue, then featured songs and dances by several cast members, including Clement and Lance. Janus and Ormelle each entered and sang their first numbers.

Finally Fitzi moved to center stage. She stuck out a hip, lusty and energetic, and did the quick cartwheel that put her in position for the long series of tricky twirls.

She breathed several times, quickly, to oxygenate her body. With a final gulp of air, she launched into the twirls. She spun with dizzying speed, while the stage and the cast rocketed by. Tiffany's face, upset now, flashed in and out of her vision.

Fitzi spun and spun and spun, better than she ever had before. She landed in a perfectly steady pose, on the far side of the stage from where she had begun, then exited quickly into the wings.

She felt high, triumphant. But her triumph wasn't quite complete yet.

She walked by Tiffany, who wore an expression of chagrin and stupefaction, and whispered casually, "It's probably just as well you dropped out, you always had so much trouble with those turns."

Tiffany gasped, furious. Fitzi danced out again to finish the scene.

Then she had a minute of intolerable suspense, but it happened as she had hoped. The second the scene was over, Tiffany sprang from the wings. Gone was the wispy Tiffany who had come into the theater just half an hour ago; gone, the frail invalid. This Tiffany was a tornado in human form, whirling out onstage, taking command.

"Ted," Tiffany called imperiously, "Could we take that scene again? I want to show Fitzi something."

"What, the whole scene?" Ted asked, bewildered.

"Please."

"Well—" He and Mr. Ettl exchanged glances. Mr. Ettl nodded, almost imperceptibly. Ted shrugged. "Okay, Tiffany."

Tiffany pulled off her boots; threw her jacket in the wings. In slacks and a shirt, and with only socks on her feet, she took Gaby's position on the stage, while Fitzi moved into the wings.

The piano player struck up the music. Mom juggled, Dad did the magic trick, Clement and Lance strutted, the chorus sang and danced. And Tiffany, as the rags-and-tatters Parisian urchin, brought Gaby to life on stage. Lusty and confident, brassy and enchanting, Tiffany danced and sang and flirted with the world.

As the scene progressed, there was rising excitement in the theater. The parents, jaded from weeks of rehearsals, even the cast and crew, were sent into a mood that almost crackled.

Then Tiffany spun into the turns, powerful, confident, an incredible dynamo. She seemed to cross the stage like a meteor, trailing stardust.

She flipped into the frozen pose at the end, her arms held high.

Fitzi started the applause. Then the cast took it up, the parents, the crew. At last even Ted and Mr. Ettl were clapping, cheering.

Tiffany's smile, her body, her whole being, seemed to shine. With her arms stretched up, it was as though she were standing onstage before a full house, on opening night.

The ovation washed over her.

·

Tiffany played the role of Gaby for the rest of the rehearsal. She wouldn't quite admit she was returning permanently, but nobody doubted it.

Mark stopped Fitzi backstage, his brown eyes warm and amused. "Tiffany tells me you talked her into coming today."

"Yes, sort of."

"You knew it would work out this way, didn't you?"

"Well, she does always rise to a challenge."

He laughed. "So do you, Fitzi. I'm glad you've got your dance back."

"Me too."

Usually so poised, Mark seemed shy suddenly. "The Museum of Modern Art's doing a dance retrospective in their film series. Would you like to go with me on Sunday?

It's Fred Astaire in *Top Hat*. Unless you'd rather do something else—"

Joy sparked in Fitzi. "There's nothing I'd rather do."

Later, as the cast was leaving the theater, Tiffany cornered her. "Let's get together Sunday. We could take in a movie."

"No. I'm going with Mark to the Museum of Modern Art. A Fred Astaire film."

"Sounds like fun," Tiffany responded airily. "I might tag along, I haven't been to MOMA in ages. Mark could pick me up." She looked around for him.

Fitzi grabbed her wrist hard, nailing her in place. "Oh, no you won't. What's yours is yours, what's mine is mine. Got that? Now buzz off." She released Tiffany's wrist.

Catered to by almost everybody since her ordeal ended, Tiffany looked as if she couldn't believe her ears. Pouting, she flounced away, speechless for once.

■

When they began rehearsing with the full orchestra, the big, rich sounds thrilled Fitzi. So did the intricate lighting, as run-throughs became almost like finished performances. Suddenly the Paris sets were more convincing; you could believe that in this fabulous city, even the craziest dream might come true.

They still weren't rehearsing in costume, but when the spotlight hit Fitzi for her dance, a switch seemed to turn her on inside, starting a deep surge of excitement. Even in old sweats, she felt as if she were wearing her street-dancer costume, ribbons on her wrists, new red tap shoes on her feet. She could hardly wait for dress rehearsals.

But as each element of the show was added, it became evident that the production was running too long, as many had feared it would. Mr. Ettl let it be known that cuts would have to be made.

Fitzi's exhilaration changed to foreboding. Act Three already had the big cabaret scene, and Clement's song, and a duet with Janus and Ormelle, and the knockout ensemble finale. She wondered miserably if it really needed her tap dance, too.

She confided her worries to Mom, who responded with shrill nervousness, "Cutting that number would be the worst mistake Seymour Ettl ever made!"

"It would be a clean cut, though," Fitzi pointed out wretchedly. "It wouldn't involve anybody but me."

Mom insisted she didn't want to hear about such foolishness. But her dark eyes shifted, restless with anxiety.

On Friday, the Wolper family arrived at rehearsal in a haze of apprehension. Only Clement, who had refused to speculate about what might happen, seemed unperturbed.

They noticed at once that the composer and choreographer were on hand, along with a couple of writers. As the rehearsal got underway, these people kept conferring with Mr. Ettl and Ted.

The cast's nerves grew tighter; some performed better than usual, some a lot worse.

When it came to her dance, Fitzi couldn't tell whether

she was great or awful. It was like auditions, all over again.

During breaks, Mr. Ettl and his associates discussed the script, occasionally scribbling on it. Finally, in the late afternoon, Mr. Ettl announced, "Okay, you're all aware we've got a problem and something has to go. Now, in Act One—"

He described cuts in the dialogue, some lines eliminated, some shortened, some phrased differently. Tiffany and Mark—and Fitzi and Jerry, their standbys—scurried to get their scripts. Most of the cuts affected them. They wrote in the altered lines, and the newly blocked moves.

"Act Two . . . ," Mr. Ettl went on.

Again dialogue was cut, but no specialty numbers.

Fitzi's stomach churned as she realized Act Three was next.

"Act Three. In the finale, we won't take that second reprise," the director decided. This meant the ensemble number would be shortened slightly. "No other change in Act Three," he ended, and Fitzi let out a long, incredulous sigh of relief.

NINETEEN

As the rehearsal broke up that afternoon, Mark said, "Fitzi, I'm sorry, we can't go to the museum on Sunday. I'll be studying my brains out."

"Yeah, I have to learn Tiffany's new stuff, too."

"Maybe next week," Mark proposed wearily. "By then, the show will have opened. The worst will be behind us."

Together they both added, "Knock wood," and burst out laughing.

Jerry Dominic passed them, his script scrunched in his hands, his face desperate. "Brother! Cut, cut, cut!" he was muttering. "I'm not sure these scenes even make *sense* anymore!"

Bernie's mother, walking by with her son, looked after Jerry, amused. "Your standby?" she asked Mark.

"Yes."

She rolled her eyes. "Stay well."

He grinned, and nodded.

.

On Sunday, Fitzi studied her changes until she could hardly focus. By the middle of the afternoon, she knew them pretty well.

The day was sunny and pleasant. Pigeons basked on the fire escape across the courtyard. She broke up some Ritz crackers for them, and spread them on her windowsill. Then she went out for a walk.

On 89th Street, she headed toward P.S. 166. Although the red brick school was only a couple of blocks from where she lived, she hadn't been there in months.

She stood on the sidewalk outside the playground, looking through the iron fence. A soft breeze brushed a few dry leaves across the pavement. A forgotten hoop, bright red, glowed like an apple in a corner.

The playground itself looked dear and small and half-forgotten. Yet this was where she had played almost every day, and she had finished sixth grade less than six months ago. She touched the iron bars, remembering Karen, freckled and laughing, hopping in a three-legged race; Pip jumping double-Dutch, her fair braid bouncing on her shoulder; and herself, Fitzi, carefree as if recess would never end.

In the hour before the curtain rose on opening night, Clement scrupulously did his voice exercises. Mom jittered through a series of good-luck rituals: marking the dressing-room mirror with her lucky lipstick, pinning her silver wishbone in her bra, repeating the *mantra* her yoga teacher had given her. Dad checked and rechecked the juggling and magic props.

Fitzi knew Karen and Pip were out front with their families. They had sent her a stuffed shark wearing sunglasses. As soon as she was dressed and made up, she stood against the wall of the dressing room, hugging the shark. She squeezed her eyes shut.

"I'm in Paris," she whispered, "and it's a beautiful day on the Champs-Élysées—"

"Places, everybody," Ted called.

Fitzi put the shark on her dressing table and drew in three calming breaths, then joined the other kids on the dim stage. In the first two acts, she was supposed to mill around with the chorus.

The orchestra struck up the overture. The curtain rose. Lights blazed. Smiles flashed. Tiffany twirled by. The street performers whisked into their acts. There was a collective sigh of pleasure from the audience as the colorful scene captivated them. They applauded sharply.

The opening action got a good response. When the balloon floated down, the scene had to stop for a solid minute of cheers and applause. Mark and Bernie and the others waited in the gondola, smiling, until the clapping subsided and Mark could ask Tiffany, "Is this Paris?"

To Fitzi, it was. She believed in this fabulous imagined place; in the odd lovers swearing "This Will Never Be a Romance"; in the jovial bartender; above all in Bistro Beau. From his first entrance, Clement bewitched the audience, drawing laughter and applause.

Fitzi shared the pervasive high mood until shortly before her dance solo. Then she was stricken with stage fright, worse than she had ever been before. The huge theater, the thousands of people, suddenly seemed like a dark monster, ready to swallow her.

What if she simply ran offstage? If she *ran,* on opening night?

Her music started. She skipped up the staircase to the top, petrified. She turned, facing the enormous audience. Below, Mom was doing her disappearing flower trick.

In every emergency of Fitzi's life, her grandfather had helped her. But now he was Bistro Beau, trading quips with the Bartender.

The spotlight hit her. As in rehearsals, Fitzi felt as though a switch had snapped on. Exactly on cue, she flung herself into her dance, red shoes tapping, ribbons flying from her wrists. She danced down the long staircase, riding on the music like a leaf on a wave. The swift little drumbeats of her taps speeded faster and faster, drawing a swelling murmur of admiration from out front. As she ended, there was a crash of applause.

She ran off. In the wings, Tiffany and Mark whispered

praise. Breathless, Fitzi nodded thanks. She turned to watch the onstage action with them.

The cabaret scene began. Dad, in white makeup and white leotard, unobtrusively mounted the staircase so he would be in place for Clement's big number.

The Parisian neon signs went out. Street performers scattered and disappeared. Bistro Beau left the cabaret. The Bartender locked up, and ambled slowly off. At the top of the staircase, the juggler silently began to toss the luminous white balls.

Clement walked to center stage. Leaning on his stick, he sang quietly, "Another evening gone, the laughter dying . . . the toasts are drunk, we've said our last goodbye . . . We want to stay—the fun passed by so quickly! . . . but we must leave, and always wonder why . . ."

As he sang verse after verse, the audience hushed, mesmerized. His pure voice rose in the final notes: "The door is locked . . . it's closing time."

Fitzi's throat closed up. Unexpected tears filmed her eyes. She blotted them carefully with her fingertips, so they wouldn't ruin her makeup.

The spotlight dimmed on her grandfather's face. Finally nothing could be seen in the darkness but the spectral figure of the juggler, keeping the white balls in the air.

·

The show was a hit. Two reviews predicted that Clement Dale would win the Tony award for best supporting actor in a musical.

Fitzi and Tiffany and their families swept off to the cast party, Fitzi's mom leading a triumphant recap of the evening's great moments.

Jubilant at how well the whole show was received, Mr. Ettl beamed at the cast. "Looks like we'll all be together for a long, long time, folks."

"Or at least until we grow taller than four ten," Fitzi whispered happily to Tiffany.